"Comes complete with Christmas spirit, kids and everything I'd need to pay my working woman's dues. *I* live in a penthouse with a housekeeper." Sam glanced around.

"Uh-huh." Dallas nodded slowly, watching his dimples creep into his cheeks.

"Well, to really make your experiment work, I'd need to feel every element of stress in the average worker's life. And I couldn't possibly get the real feeling of home life at my place."

Dallas felt her insides flutter.

Leaning his head back against the cushions of her sofa, Sam said, "If I *were* to live in an average house—say something like this—I could get the full effect. What if I spend my month of hardship here, Dallas? With you. You can keep an eye on me that way...see that I don't cheat," he added in his sexy southern drawl.

Dear Reader:

Happy Holidays from all of us at Silhouette Desire!
This is our favorite time of year, so we've pulled
together a wonderful month of love stories that are
our gifts to you, our readers.

We start out with *Man of the Month* Luke Branson
in Joan Hohl's *Handsome Devil*, which is also a
sequel to *The Gentleman Insists*, February 1989's
Man of the Month.

Also, look for three wonderful stories filled with the
spirit of the season: *Upon A Midnight Clear* by
Laura Leone, *The Pendragon Virus* by Cait London
and *Glory, Glory* by Linda Lael Miller. Rounding
out December are the delightful *Looking For
Trouble* by Nancy Martin and the tantalizing *The
Bridal Price* by Barbara Boswell. All together, these
six books might make great presents for yourself—or
perhaps for a loved one!

So enjoy December's Silhouette Desire books. And
as for 1991 . . . well, we have some wonderful plans in
store—including another year of exciting *Man of the
Month* stories! But more on all that in the new year.
In the meantime, I wish each and every one of you
the warmest seasons greetings.

All the best,

Lucia Macro
Senior Editor

CAIT LONDON
THE PENDRAGON VIRUS

SILHOUETTE *Desire*®

Published by Silhouette Books New York

America's Publisher of Contemporary Romance

SILHOUETTE BOOKS
300 East 42nd St., New York, N.Y. 10017

ISBN: 0-373-05611-7

First Silhouette Books printing December 1990

Books by Cait London

Silhouette Desire

The Loving Season #502
Angel vs. MacLean #593
The Pendragon Virus #611

CAIT LONDON

lives in the Missouri Ozarks but grew up in Washington and still loves craggy mountains and the Pacific coast. She's a full-time secretary, a history buff and an avid reader who knows her way around computers. She grew up painting—landscapes and wildlife—but is now committed to writing and enjoying her three creative daughters. Cait has big plans for her future—learning to fish, taking short trips for research and meeting people. She also writes as Cait Logan and has won *Romantic Times*' Best New Romance Writer award for 1986.

For the Ozark Romance Authors,
my RWA group, of Springfield, Missouri.
They teach love and inspire with a kindness
that reaches into the lives they touch.
For them, and you, my friends, Merry Christmas.

One

———

Sam Loring had one basic rule: locate the problem and get to the bottom of it—quick. Easing his six-foot-four frame on the folding metal chair, he crossed his arms over his chest. He surveyed the conference room with the air of a fighter who had come to study his opponent.

Rain tapped at the windows, the sound seeming gentler than the chatter surrounding him. The cold bite of the rain was typical of Seattle weather in early December and suited Sam's mood. Skimming the thirty faces of the class members, he spotted the one on the advertising brochure. Focusing on her, Sam took a deep breath. Dallas Pendragon needed to be taken out of the game—his game.

Youthful male executives peppered the predominantly female class. The fact that Sam was the only older man in a room of excited women didn't bother him at all. His staff at Brice Cleansers Company was coming down with a contagious business virus, and he intended to stop it. Christmas season or not.

He ran his palm across his flat stomach, easing the threatening ache. Remembering his morning business call, he scowled. A competitor had almost ripped a contract out from under his nose, and Sam had spent the better part of his morning angling to undercut the low bid. Wooing the buyer had cost him a precious morning hour.

Sam rotated his tense shoulders slowly. His sales team captain had been too eager to get the contract for commercial washroom soap. Johnson had missed presenting an important feature of the dispenser to the buyer. The mistake wouldn't be repeated, Sam thought grimly. He'd called Johnson on the carpet at seven this morning.

Sliding an antacid tablet from his suit pocket, Sam ground it between his teeth. At forty-six, he'd survived a nasty divorce and a few corporate battles. Along the way, he'd buried an Appalachian Southern drawl and rebuilt a sagging company.

He tugged at his collar, loosening it slightly around the tense cords of his neck. He could survive the Pendragon virus.

Pendragon, the inventive owner and lecturer of a business-stress school, had damn near incited a mutiny in his staff of two hundred workers. The best portion of his staff at Brice were loyal, trained professionals. But somehow Pendragon had whipped his smooth waters into a tidal wave. She was a firebrand oozing karma, he decided darkly, watching the tall, lithe woman step up to the stage.

Pendragon had just enough age—late thirties—on her to be dangerous, he decided. The crusading age.

Tracing the strong clean line of her jaw, Sam shifted in his chair uncomfortably. Pendragon had *professional woman* written all over her; it was a species he meticulously avoided.

He could almost feel her electricity from his seat in midclass. With a traveling microphone attached to her pinstriped navy blazer, she dominated the room. Sam could feel it—the Pendragon virus—crackle, lashing at him.

Her hair just touched her shoulders, swaying as she walked across the portable stage, preparing for her lecture.

The strands shifted as she turned, a sleek sensuous movement of silk on silk. With hair the color of burnished copper, she probably had a temper to match.

Quickly stacking a variety of pamphlets and tapes across a table, Pendragon paused to check her wristwatch, then continued her preparations. Sam shifted his weight uneasily, noting her professional conduct.

Pendragon was a long-legged witch, her skirt tightening as she strode across the stage to adjust the microphone stand. She had the loose stride of an athlete rather than a woman who kept her bottom plopped in a desk chair.

Sam watched as she took a moment to scan Seattle's downtown business area from the conference-room window. He studied that pale profile intently as Pendragon's slim, ringless finger gently rubbed the bridge of her nose. He recognized that trick—preparing for a presentation. Do your best to prepare, take a minute before showtime to center in on yourself, then give 'em your best shot.

He also recognized his own flash of admiration for her; Pendragon was a pro.

She lifted her head slightly, and a thick strand of hair slid to frame her face. The wave caressed her smooth cheek, then arched to expose the tiny diamond stud nestled in her ear. For some reason, Sam found that twinkling stone entirely too intriguing; his gaze was fastened upon it. The muscles of his neck tightened in an instinctive, self-protective gesture.

The small stone was too feminine, the curve of her lobe too vulnerable. Sam rapped a pencil against his palm impatiently.

Her face lighting, Pendragon spoke to a woman who had approached the stage. The lecturer listened intently, her mouth curving with a smile. Watching her, a chill ran up the nape of Sam's neck. Her full lips had the look of ripe strawberries, and he could almost feel them opening—

Damn, he thought, forcing his gaze through the window to Seattle's famous waterfront street, bordered by shops and eateries.

If ever there was a woman he didn't want to experience sensually, it was the steel-in-silk type. Career women could cut a man in two, then walk over the pieces.

Sam slipped another antacid tablet into his mouth. When he wanted a woman, he liked lace and a lot of soft, comforting curves. But lately he hadn't found anything that had even tempted his tastes.

At promptly nine o'clock, Pendragon turned center stage and flashed a thousand-watt smile at the class. Thirty women stopped chattering and sat at attention, gripping their training manuals. In contrast, the young male executives looked wary.

Sam traced the manual's bold letters of the Pendragon Method of Handling Business Stress with his pen. He underlined the topic for handling difficult bosses, feeling the muscles in his jaw contract. He wanted—demanded—an efficient work force. But after his staff had attended Pendragon's one-day course, they had him under a microscope. His employees' curious glances and closed expressions had sent Sam's primed senses tingling.

For the past week, he'd waded through problems created by Pendragon's business-slash-stress school. Personnel had sent him a cute little notice: "Abnormal amount of requests for To-Whom-It-May-Concern job recommendations. Also requests for job record updates... Anything Personnel needs to know?"

If an employee suddenly wanted his personnel file updated, it usually meant he or she was job shopping, and that spelled trouble. An efficiency survey had revealed that it took a minimum of three years to train a good employee. If any one of the cogs were displaced—

The pencil Sam had been holding snapped between his fingers. Sam scowled at the usurper. Troublemakers came in all sorts of shapes and sizes, and there was always a way to put them out of commission.

For the past week, he'd been waiting for the employee virus to run its course. Emily Franzini, his personal secretary, hadn't had his morning coffee waiting for the first time in eleven years. Nor had she waited, quiet and with pen in hand, while he examined his morning mail. Then, as he had rummaged for a fitting business threat to close a letter, Emily had politely suggested he try a dictation recorder to save them both time.

Feeling confined, Sam rolled his broad shoulders against the back of the conference chair. He liked his morning coffee on his desk when he arrived and he didn't like dictating to a machine. Emily had quoted a high percentage of managers who possessed the marvelous ability, then had looked down her nose at him. "I'm merely suggesting an alternative. Ms. Pendragon says that offering helpful suggestions is a way to relieve stress. It gives one such a good, warm feeling to be helpful... Ah, did you know you've been dictating for an hour straight?" she had asked, flexing her fingers.

Sam leveled a dark stare at Pendragon, the proponent of taking regular breaks to alleviate stress. So he'd gotten wrapped up in his dictation; so he didn't catch Emily shifting restlessly in her chair after an hour. He liked Emily, but once he got started on a marketing analysis, his ideas were fresh and he wanted them written down. So he forgot sometimes.

Sam winced quietly, feeling guilty. He worked hard, pounding at problems until he'd tenderized the gristle. It was just that sometimes he forgot that Emily's fingers might ache. If he'd realized— Sam shifted on his chair, feeling guiltier.

In the middle of his dictation, Emily had glanced longingly at his private coffeepot, and Sam realized he had worked through her break. To compensate for his thoughtlessness, Sam had foolishly asked if Emily had any ideas about improving his relations with the staff. She had quietly suggested that he not greet his personal clerical staff each morning with "Hi, girls." Then she'd added, "They are trained professionals, Mr. Loring. Businesspersons, according to the Pendragon theory."

His staff was the blood of his business, Sam thought darkly, and he didn't need any interference from Pendragon.

Morrison Bradley, a friend and an executive from Delite's Pet Food Company, had called on Tuesday, raving. "No rush jobs, my staff says, Sam. I've got a memo in my hand from the employee representative who runs the suggestion program in the loading and delivery departments. We're out to sell cat and dog food here. How do the employees expect us to get the products on the top shelf without rush jobs? Scheduling cuts employee stress, they say. We do the same thing every year and they want routine projects scheduled by the month. Damn, in the old days workers did what you threw at 'em. When you threw it at 'em!"

Over lunch on Wednesday, Mort Radney was grim. "My secretaries either treat me like a child or they're too damned busy to talk. Nelson, my chief, had the nerve to say that they react that way when I'm moody.... Moody," he repeated indignantly. "He says they have feelings, too. 'They're people, for Pete's sake,' he said."

On the stage, Pendragon adjusted the microphone attached to her lapel. "Can you all hear me? Raise your hands if you can't."

Noting her slight Western twang, Sam concentrated on the husky undertone.

"Good. Everything is working fine then. Good morning, I'm Dallas Pendragon," she began, walking across the stage and displaying a neat length of leg beneath the slim skirt.

Dallas Pendragon, troublemaker, Sam thought. She had just the right combination to stir his clerical workers into a potential mutiny—she was bright and in total control of herself. The ultimate businessperson, Sam thought darkly, scanning the way the slim skirt fitted her neat backside.

"Make sure you're wearing your name tag," she instructed with another wide smile. "By the end of the day, we're all going to know each other well."

Introducing herself as a divorced working mother who knew about coping with stress and business, Dallas slid right into the office workers' hearts. Sam got the feeling that the woman was a bully. She liked having things her way.

He liked having things *his* way: without the clutter of day-care centers and job-sharing positions. Career women were fine—at a distance. But once they started mothering children on company time....

Sam's gaze strolled down her slender body appraisingly. He had to take her out of the game without too many bruises, he decided—only because it wouldn't look good for someone with his size to shove her into a corner.

When she instructed the class to turn to their booklets, Sam leveled a hard scowl at her. He paid his people well, tagging on bonuses, vacations and maternity leave. If Ms. Pendragon wasn't stopped soon, every business in Seattle would be footing the bill for day-care center accommodations and fitness gyms.

By the midmorning break, Sam knew he was right to experience Ms. Pendragon first hand. If she hadn't been his opponent, he would have admired her quick wit, which reached straight into the hearts of working women.

As a man who appreciated women, Sam couldn't help comparing her to his past collection of females. Pendragon dressed like sheer business and she probably wore practical cotton panties.

He edged his way through the crowd gathering at the coffeepot, just catching hints of "She's right. There's absolutely no reason not to have some kind of day-care center arrangement at work." And "I agree. A fit, healthy person does make a good worker. Diet is important. The company should provide a microwave oven."

One comment snagged and chafed. "I just can't wait to get back to work and get started on these new ideas. According to the Pendragon theory, it's important to analyze your boss. Study his needs and yours. Then go for a compromise... Or as a last resort, think about moving into another workplace that better suits you."

Sam scowled at the coffee urn. When he was twelve years old, he was working as a man to survive. Because he'd known genuine gnawing hunger, he paid top wages for good workers. As an employer, he didn't want to be compromised. Or feel like a lump of clay to be pushed and prodded into the employee's idea of a manager. And he didn't want his workers looking around for other jobs.

Hell, he liked his workers. Most of them had been with the company for years and had been perfectly happy until *The Virus* had gotten to them.

A blond woman with long, carefully mussed hair and heavily kohled eyes tracked him as he moved through the crowd. Accustomed to the knowing look, he nodded just as a short woman accidentally brushed his sleeve with her large bosom.

Edging past a sea of conflicting scents and chattering women, Sam finally reached his seat. Buffeted by the excitement racing around the room, he gripped the back of the chair like an anchor.

His stomach felt like hell.

"I liked the part about some companies having a sabbatical program after a five-year employment. A longer vacation would really be nice, like a present from the company," he heard as he slid back into his chair, coffee in hand.

A plump woman seated next to him leaned over and smiled knowingly. "Isn't the Pendragon concept great? I really liked the part about maybe not being in the right job . . . a square peg in a round hole. I mean if the company is going to treat workers like yesterday's newspaper, why not look around?"

Yesterday's newspaper. Sam repeated the phrase in a quiet snarl. He packed in a good, long work day and never asked as much of his people as of himself. His staff had the best of equipment to help manage their work loads, and he'd instituted top training programs. He wanted to keep his expert people, not have them shopping for other jobs. If Pendragon kept up at this rate, the entire Seattle clerical workforce would be in constant rotation.

When Pendragon stepped up to the stage, the cords running down Sam's neck went taut. He adjusted his black-rimmed glasses meticulously. He'd worked damned hard to establish a management-and-labor committee. Brice provided insurance, counseling for alcoholics and an hour-long Christmas party.

He'd written a manual for Brice employees defining goals, procedures and personal conduct. His managers had an open-door policy for employee problems and the latitude to handle them.

A thin woman leaned across him to speak to the lady on his other side. "Wouldn't it be great if management provided free counseling? I've got a teenage son who really resents his stepfather—"

"Okay, let's hit it!" Pendragon exclaimed enthusiastically, raising her arm. To Sam her wrist looked as though he could wrap his fingers around the pale column, and he felt a warning, cold trickle run up his neck. For just a moment, Sam allowed himself a glimpse of her soft curves beneath the business suit. He narrowed his eyes, settling back for another dose of the Pendragon virus.

A hotshot dynamo concealed in skirts and pantyhose, he thought. Ready to take the whole business world on to prove her theories. The next segment dealt with analyzing your boss, stroking his needs and getting what you want. While the class studiously checked off the personality type of their bosses and themselves, Sam studied Pendragon.

She would have made a great coach for major-league football, a female Gipper. An exciting speaker, Pendragon could toss off a quick joke at the same time she eased a shy woman into talking.

Unused to sitting for any length of time, Sam stirred in his chair. Pendragon scouted the crowd, then her eyes snagged on him. "Now that gentleman has the right idea."

Walking to him, Pendragon smiled. Just a mere lifting of one corner of her full lips. Sam had a glimpse of dark green eyes framed by sweeping lashes. He didn't trust the sparkling, gold flecked depths. They were witch's eyes.

"Time to stir up the oxygen level in the blood, people," she announced, reading his name tag. "Sam is going to show us how to exercise. Okay, Sam? Stand up," she ordered briskly.

Sam breathed heavily just once. He didn't like being hauled around like a schoolboy. Apparently Pendragon expected her orders to be followed because she tapped him lightly on one broad shoulder. A fine dark eyebrow arced high. "Coming, Sam?"

Rising slowly, Sam stood to his full height, noting that Pendragon in her practical pumps reached his chin. He also noted a delicate scent of flowers that reminded him of Georgia's Appalachia hills blooming in May. Or maybe it was his mother's sweet peas by the shack's back door.

Pendragon strode around him like a general studying an imposing fort before she addressed the class. "Okay. Here you have a sizeable man. You should all be able to see him well enough. Roll your head around like this, Sam. Loosens the shoulder and neck muscles."

Lifting her hands, she placed them just behind Sam's ears and rotated his head gently. "Think you can handle that, Sam?" she asked in a teasing tone.

Sam ground his teeth together.

The position of her body near his was a trespass. When he wanted a woman touching him, *he* reached out and snagged her. She rubbed the taut cords in his neck soothingly, watching him for just that slice of an instant. "You really should relax, Sam," she offered gently.

Relax? How the hell did a man do that when a woman's soft hands were strolling all over him? In Sam's book of man-woman rules, the intimacy wasn't performed in front of a crew of women!

The soft curve of her breasts brushed his midsection as she guided his head, and Sam stiffened. "Relax, Sam. Close your eyes," she whispered, continuing the motion. "Easy... easy..."

"I can manage now," he returned a little gruffly. He was all too aware of her sweet-pea, down-home fragrance and the soft curves almost touching his body. Suddenly, he realized the impact of her hands. He hadn't been touched by a woman for some time, and now he was bordering a sensual discussion with the needs of his body!

"Okay, then do it by yourself." Her hands slid from him, and Sam felt just a twinge of regret.

But how much regret could he spend on a danger to his company? he wondered.

After Sam obeyed stiffly, Pendragon ran him through a series of stretching exercises, then called, "Minnie, would you bring a stool for Sam so he can relax for our next exercise?"

Noting the long wave of hair that coursed down her cheek, he had the urge to sweep it back from her face. She had one of those everlasting faces—the dark lifted eyebrows and high cheekbones and a short pert nose.

A nose dusted with freckles.

He glanced uneasily at her throat. He could almost wrap his hand around it. The pad of his thumb would just fit in the hollow at the base of her throat.

Pendragon leisurely appraised his navy suit and light blue shirt. "From the looks of him, this guy requires exercise. He's probably used to movement and works out somehow. So we know he's in pretty good shape...." Her eyes drifted to Sam's lean midsection. "Basically."

A small flick of pique raced through him. If she wanted to find a soft gut, she could look somewhere else. His backside wasn't flabby, either.

She tugged the tall stool closer. "Sit down, Sam. You're our guinea pig for biofeedback. That's it," she said as he settled on the stool, "get really comfortable, then hold absolutely still so the feedback device won't pick up the sound of your clothing."

The softness of her breast brushed his sleeve, and Sam scowled, edging away from her.

Patting his shoulder, she flashed a grin up at him. "You're a good guy, Sam." Tilting the microphone away from her mouth, Pendragon whispered, "Since you're the only older man in class, I really appreciate your help. The younger guys probably don't have the sedentary job you may have, so they're not as good as examples. You know, less chance of heart problems, circulatory and so forth. I think it's important for women to see that older... middle-age men experience real stress, too. Thanks."

When she turned to the class, Sam shot a grim look down her backside. It was all there—the curves and the strength. Too bad it was wasted on a female shark. He hadn't volunteered; he'd been drafted. And he didn't like being patronized, either. Or called old. Or put on the spot to be dissected by twenty women and a few men.

She placed her hand on his sleeve. The slim pale fingers that squeezed his forearm had practical short nails. "We all have stress of some kind or another. Sometimes we recognize it immediately and other times we have to work at it. That's what this is for—" She held up a small wand. "This is a biofeedback monitor. Listen to the tone when I place it in Sam's hand."

When he took the monitor from her, his fingers slid along hers deliberately, testing her skin. Immediately Pendragon sliced a quick appraisal at him.

Instantly the amplifiers from her microphone picked up a high whine that seemed to hover like a raindrop clinging to the tip of a leaf.

She smiled briefly, clinically pleased by the demonstration. "Hear that, class? Sam's excited. Now listen to the tone as we talk. In areas that might be stressful to Sam, the pitch will rise."

Whipping around, she placed her hand on her hip studying him closely. "Sam's here to learn, so he's going to appreciate finding out for free about his private stress areas. This is helpful in the office place. If you can afford to buy the machine, take it to work. You'll find that things you didn't know bothered you are really stressful. And then you can deal with them.''

Sam closed his eyes. The tone rose to a high whine as he thought of each of his employees holding one of the damned devices. The class giggled, but Pendragon only nodded.

"Okay, there's something causing Sam stress. Are you nervous?''

Sam wanted to crush the deceiving little device in his hand. Instead he pushed his lips back from his teeth to form a smile. "A little.''

"It's only natural,'' she responded gently, patting his upper arm. "Don't worry. If things get too bad, I'll let you off the hook.''

Her tone caused him to grip the device tighter. It cried out loudly. He wanted to toss it out the window. "I can manage,'' he stated between his teeth.

Patting him on the shoulder, Pendragon purred, "That's great.'' When she continued looking straight into him, a high whine penetrated the room. Sam breathed deeply, willing the damned thing to fail. He could feel her ticking off his emotional problems.

Okay, he admitted almost guiltily to himself. He was basically a private person. He didn't like grave diggers prowling around in his psyche.

"Settle down,'' Pendragon whispered, covering her microphone. "You're off the charts. Now let's just chat so the class can hear the different tones ... Nothing too intimate, I promise.'' She smiled briefly and Sam caught the gleam of even white teeth.

The sound settled down to a steady hum as Pendragon swished around him, addressing the class. "These devices are really great. Hold them while you watch television. To deal with stress, you must first recognize it. Doing okay, Sam?''

"Great,'' he responded, pleased that the tone had settled somewhat.

She nodded. "You look like a man who knows himself pretty well," she began, her gaze following his broken nose and thrusting jaw.

"Pretty well," he agreed, realizing his palm had just begun to sweat as it cradled the humming device.

"Do you have a family, Sam?"

"No."

"Potential family? As in fianceé, stepchildren?"

Sam heard the threatening hum raise slightly. Pendragon caught the sound and smiled knowingly. "We're all friends here, Sam . . . trying to learn about ourselves. Do you want to explain?" she asked almost gently.

Damn it! No, he didn't want to explain—the tone raised and quivered throughout the room. His work was both his child and his mistress. He gripped the tattletale monitor tightly.

Okay, so he had an occasional long night. In fact, he dreaded the upcoming holidays when his friends and staff would be celebrating with their families. He just never seemed to fit in and hated the awkward feeling. "No one," he admitted through the line of his teeth as the humming increased.

"Ah, you see how well the device works, class? Sam, for some reason, is upset. You see, this is a typical stress point. Families can create as well as ease stress for a business person. It's all in how that individual manages problems. Sharing problems with a loved one is one of the best ways to ease tension. They're on your team, wanting to help. And that's good for us. Let's hope Sam gets that break one day."

Dallas placed her hand on Sam's arm deliberately. The man was literally grinding his teeth. A classic workaholic, she decided, noting the strong muscles shifting beneath her touch.

Sam Loring was the size of a mountain. He had a hard look, with searing gray eyes and ferocious thick brows. His neatly clipped hair just touched with silver, did little to soften his image.

If ever there was a man who needed lessons in dealing with stress, it was Sam. His biofeedback sound was abnormally high. No wonder, she thought, unconsciously squeezing his forearm. No family and all alone during the holidays.

When she'd moved his head in the rotation exercise, she could feel his basic resistance to guidance. As a "touching" person, Dallas could almost read personalities through her fingertips. Sam was of the unbending variety, driven and badly needing softening.

In the exercise, she had caught his soapy scent. Sam wouldn't be too bad with his rough edges trimmed, she decided. Dallas rather liked the battered-old-tom image she sensed beneath his stiff exterior.

And she had liked touching him, feeling the rough masculine muscles beneath her fingertips. His dark brown hair was nice, sliding easily through her fingers. The course, defiant texture was no doubt representative of the man.

Dallas left her hand on Sam's arm as she ran him through a simple series of questions that seemed to upset him unreasonably. He had a raspy, deep voice that for some unknown reason could lift the hair at the back of her neck. A scar ran into the dark hair at his temple, which made him look all the more tough and serious. Dallas wondered if he knew how to laugh.

She smiled at him, willing him to know he had a friend in the world; for the moment she could spare Sam a little warmth. As she chatted with him, Dallas noted the high whine of the monitor. For some reason, Sam Loring was unjustifiably emotional!

Sympathetic to his loneliness during the impending holiday season, Dallas ended the session quickly and ordered the afternoon break. Taking the monitor from Sam's big hand, she noted the scars across his knuckles. Dallas smiled up at him as he stood. "Thank you so much, Sam. I hope you're enjoying the training session."

His lips moved, pressing together before he leaned down slightly. The lines between his eyebrows and framing his mouth deepened. "I want to talk with you privately, Ms. Pendragon."

She stepped back from him. Sam's gray eyes slashed at her. "I have counselors available, Sam. Call the office for an appointment—"

"Not them. *You* Pendragon," he demanded in a tone that reminded her of her dog's low, menacing growl.

That slight touch of arrogance erased her sympathy for Sam's loneliness. His do-it-or-else tone also reminded her of her ex-husband when he was shoving his weight around.

T. J. McCall had been totally unsympathetic to her pressures. An overgrown boy, T.J. was frequently out of work. He had no understanding about her budding career and did nothing to contribute to their home and children.

Dallas *really* disliked that tone.

She wrapped the cord of the monitor neatly around the device and returned it to the box. She turned slowly, facing him. "Exactly what do you want, Sam?"

He glanced around at the curious women as though surveying enemy territory. "I'd like to talk with you. As soon as possible."

"Talk now," she stated, glancing at her wristwatch. She'd had enough of one man demanding and setting the restraints on her time. "We've got ten minutes left of the break."

Sam shot an angry look down at her—a man nettled by obeying someone else's rules. He rubbed his jaw with the flat of his hand. "What I've got in mind will take more time."

Dallas was in no mood to delicately handle a come-on from a man who looked hard as nails. She'd had a rough work week, made worse by her children coming down with flu. Besides, her mother had renewed her attack on Dallas's no-man status. According to Lisa Pendragon, every woman needed a good man now and then to keep her in fighting shape for the next one. Or she suggested, Dallas might try harder to capture one of the basic, dull variety.

It was Lisa who had gently but firmly informed Dallas that T.J. wasn't what she called "a real man." When Dallas stopped running long enough to take a slow, thorough look at their relationship, she found T.J. to be a spoiled child, more demanding than Nikki and Billy.

Dallas glanced up at Sam's tough jawline, taking in the heavy shadow of his beard. Somehow she suspected he wasn't dull. He had that elemental look that would please her mother, but just didn't suit herself. "Give me a rough idea, Sam."

He didn't like anyone setting conditions but himself, she noted as the muscle running the length of his cheek contracted. "I run Brice Cleansers, Ms. Pendragon. Some of my people took a class from you. The suggestion was from my personnel office, and I agreed to the company footing the bill for your contract. I now regret that decision."

"Exactly what is your complaint?"

"You've got my work force in an uproar," he stated flatly, leaning down toward her. "If you'll admit to them that all this stress analysis is malarkey, we can get back in running shape for the new year."

Dallas lifted her chin, remembering instantly the comments from Sam's employees. Though he paid well, Sam expected his people to work every bit as hard as himself. It wasn't unusual for him to call an employee or an entire work group back on Saturday morning to iron out production problems. Sam's problem wasn't in providing an overtime paycheck; it was in considering an employee's private commitments.

Under Sam's management, all employees were full-time workers with benefits provided such as insurance and paid major holidays. There were designated vacation periods determined by the company. This arrangement sometimes caused workers married to "outsiders" to have conflicting schedules.

Several Brice comment sheets stated that the employees were considering leaving the company because of the no part-timer policy. With babies and small children, the women really wanted to work half days until they could return full time. Other companies were looking into job sharing, but Brice remained rigid.

One middle-aged woman with slight medical problems wished that Brice would offer an exercise room available during her lunch hour.

Five years ago, Dallas had learned, Sam had decided that the Brice offices needed updating and had contracted a professional decorator. Given a variety of designs, Sam had selected a sterile, masculine one with ultramodern furniture and huge artificial plants. He'd promptly issued a memo that he didn't want the sleek offices "garbaged up by cutesy personal mementoes or made into a living-plant jungle." Two Brice workers had commented on the "cold" working environment, wanting living plants and pictures of their families.

While Brice provided training, the managers, backed by Sam, rarely listened to what the employees had learned from the sessions.

She also remembered the women's evaluation sheets for their boss. On paper, their composite opinions formed a hard-driving man who spent little time and attention on matters concerning other people's emotions. Loring ran the company by the book— his personal manual for profit. He spent no time considering anything but productivity. Loring did not take time to chat nor to take subtle hints.

One worker, while stating that Brice offered an excellent program for advancement, bonuses, grievances and harassments, gifted Sam with the tag, "a human machine."

"Your people were very excited about my ideas, Sam. I remember their comments specifically. Several of them were already discussing presenting ideas for day-care accommodation. They were relieved to know that I thought care centers would help their job performance."

"Uh-huh." He looked down his broken nose at her, the picture of male arrogance. "I run a profitable multimillion-dollar business, Pendragon. Complete with stockholders and board meetings. We have quality products and quality workers—"

"Why are they unhappy then, Sam?" she interrupted, feeling her anger rise. She remembered one specific complaint from a Brice worker: *I've been rated down on a messy desk at the company. Yet I'm the most creative, productive employee in our branch. At the end of the day, I place my files neatly in a stack. I know where everything is, too.*

Apparently, Brice wanted its workers to be neat, thoughtless robots, Dallas decided. And the man standing before her was the cause.

He narrowed his eyes, shifting his weight over his spread legs in a typical fighter's stance. "So far as I know, they aren't unhappy."

She arced an eyebrow, confident that she had her own fighting skills. "Have you been listening?"

He didn't like that shot. The muscles in his neck tightened as they ran into his expensive dress shirt. "Of course, I listen," he snapped, hooking a finger inside his collar to unbutton it. He tugged loose his tie. "I'm not the only employer experiencing problems over your classes. Suddenly good employees are beginning to question perfectly good, standard management practices. We're drowning in silly suggestions about this stress nonsense."

Dallas tilted her head to one side, studying Sam's dark face. "So you decided to check out the problem and attend my class in the flesh. I had hoped you were attending to learn something—"

"Lady, you are pushing. If you keep preaching this stress garbage—"

"Ah, you think your realm is threatened and you're not open to new ideas. In the first place, I'm not trying to start trouble. But stress management concerns most people and I'm merely trying to help people find ways to deal with it. Your stress level is so high, you nearly throttled the biofeedback monitor. Yet you won't concede that this is something that effects a workplace. I'd call that closed thinking," she volleyed back. Dallas normally didn't spend time fighting lost causes. But she deeply resented that she had been feeling sympathetic toward him earlier.

"I run my company how I see fit," he said between his teeth.

"So did Attila the Hun. Class will resume soon. I suggest you take your seat and learn a few things about opening your mind. For your own well being and for your employees."

When his eyes darkened and he leaned down toward her as though readying another attack, she lifted her head. "You have my number, call me when you're in a better mood. But for now, I'm in control of this class and you will either leave or take your seat. Though you probably won't chose the latter. You might not have the guts for it."

Two

―――

"You've just finished your second piece of chocolate pie, Dallas dear. Shouldn't you let that settle before you eat the popcorn you're planning?" Dallas's mother asked that evening. Lisa frequently used the guest bedroom, especially when she sensed her daughter was on edge. Tonight, Dallas appreciated the gesture, valuing Lisa as a parent and as a friend. An encounter with Sam Loring would upset anyone.

Curled up on the other end of the couch and dressed in scarlet satin pajamas, Lisa studied Dallas's worn, tight jeans and sweatshirt. "Of course you burn off the calories faster than they can lodge on your bones. Especially when you're in the crusading mood. Oh, don't look at me like that—I recognize the look."

Nikki looked up from her coloring book, spread before the television set. Only six years old, she could almost read her mother's moods. "Grandma, Mommy looks just like the time the store took too much candy money from me."

Billy stopped studying the Christmas tree's twinkling lights. He snuggled next to Dallas, wrapping his arms around her tightly. "Mommy," he muttered sleepily. "Hold me."

Kissing the top of his head, Dallas drew the sturdy four-year-old to her lap. She nuzzled Billy's hair, kissing his cheek. Nikki and Billy were the best and only things T.J. had given her.

She'd been twenty-nine and was just beginning her career as a management-employee consultant when she married T.J. At the time, T.J. was the most dazzling man she'd ever met, sweeping her out of years of serious studies and dull, exhausting office routines. Maybe she'd been subconsciously looking for an escape, and a tall, virile athletic office manager was just the white knight she'd been seeking. Though he protested her keeping her maiden name, T.J. was an elegant groom in a fairy-tale wedding.

She hadn't spent time delving into sexuality prior to her marriage, and T.J. offered a tempting, blinding initiation. Part of T.J.'s appeal was that he needed her . . . to help him meet deadlines, to balance his staff's budget and to care for him. T.J. liked being taken care of so well that he retired from the working world within one year of their marriage.

With the passing of time, Dallas realized that her love for T.J. wasn't deep or lasting.

While Dallas struggled to keep a dying marriage afloat in a reality of exhaustion, arguments and unpaid bills, she became pregnant with Nikki. The unborn baby nestling within her gave Dallas what she had been seeking—the peace of motherhood.

T.J. was aghast and outraged. While Dallas struggled with a demanding career, an apartment, a baby and a childish husband, she accidentally became pregnant with Billy. Now she realized that her last attempts at pleasing T.J. were made to ease her feeling of failure. Then T.J. walked out, signing away his parental rights with a sigh of relief— "Sorry, babe. I'm not spending my life wrapped up in kids. You're making enough money, and you know what the judge said about

me taking a hike if I didn't pay support. That's fine with me:
I won't be back."

Nikki was hers alone then, and her life was, too. With a
fierce dedication, and in early months of pregnacy, Dallas
began restructuring her life.

She had wanted a home for her children. Five years ago,
she'd haunted the Seattle suburbs to find the snug two-story
house. With a tiny garden and a gnarled old apple tree, the
house had charm from its shutters to its wooden shingles.
Built at the turn of the century with cedar timber, the house
had its ailments. But Dallas enjoyed puttering and painting
when she could and playing in the rose garden. She had just
settled in when Billy was born.

Now, draped with holiday wreaths, the house sported a
mistletoe ball over the couch—an area designated by the
children for "easy kissing." The scents of holiday baking
blended with the tangy essence of a simmering potpourri
pot.

Lisa's still-beautiful face warmed as Nikki stopped coloring and came to sit against her. The older woman put the
glamour magazine aside to place her arm around the little
girl. "Your mother has that fighting gleam in her eyes,
honey. She was like that at your age—when she beat up
Freddie Linsey for tormenting a kitten. He was twice her
size, but she was outraged. If she could just decide to fight
for a man as hard as she does for her causes, we might get
you a daddy."

"Mother, don't give Nikki any ideas. Just because you
think a man is the solution to every problem. . . ." Dallas
protested lovingly. At sixty plus, her mother was widowed
and socially active. A petite blonde, she danced until dawn
and thrived on romance. Lisa appreciated and frequently
sampled a promising male confection; she saw no reason
why Dallas couldn't do the same.

Lisa's eyes sparkled. "Since when have men become ob-
solete? Dear, there are just some things you can't do
alone. . . . Why, just the other day, I saw this marvelous peignoir set and I thought if you would just let go a little—"

"Mother, would you please wait until the children are in bed?"

From her end of the couch, Lisa grinned impishly. "You'll tell me all about it then, of course?"

"Mommy," Billy murmured. "Pauly's daddy fights the bears out of his room."

Dallas rocked his warm little body against her, kissing his drooping eyelids. "Why, honey, I do that. Every night. Your room is bear-proofed."

She kissed his soft cheek. Billy burrowed closer and she tucked the blanket around him. He yawned, lifting a chubby hand to lazily toy with her hair. His other hand rubbed a tattered satin blanket. "But Pauly's daddy shaves every morning. And carries him around on his shoulders.... I want a daddy for Christmas." With another yawn, the little boy drifted off into sleep in her arms.

"He's such a baby," Nikki whispered with a lofty tone as she disappeared into the kitchen.

Grinning at Dallas, Lisa asked. "A work problem, perhaps? It surely couldn't be a man," she teased. "I may have to buy that snazzy peignoir myself."

"Mother, as it happens, the problem is both work related and a man. A very big man, with a bigger problem."

"Mmm, my, that sounds promising. I'm glad I decided to spend the night here instead of my apartment," Lisa cooed. "I'm waiting to hear what he looks like. Anything I'd be interested in? Or maybe you'd like to join me in my belly-dancing class just to shape up those unused muscles."

Dallas went still, remembering every moment of her confrontation with Sam Loring. "He's big and tough right to his bones. Absolutely blind to the problems of a worker's stress. He has no conception of how to manage a home and a family. Or what the company could do to cut absenteeism."

Lisa raised her eyebrows. "Mmm. Repeat the big-and-tough part. I like it. Come on, give. I'll bet he's one of those yummy macho men with muscles and a nice, tight tush. How old? Is he married?"

"He's not married or anything close," Dallas muttered, remembering the biofeedback experiment. How could she have felt so sorry for that unbending piece of chauvinistic male? "There's not much market these days for a dictator."

"And looks? Was he macho or just one of those wimps that you seem to attract?"

Dallas straightened her shoulders. "There was absolutely nothing wrong with Douglas."

"Well, he certainly wasn't bedroom material. The man was a cold fish if ever I saw one," Lisa returned adamantly. "I don't believe any man has really lit your fire, not even T.J. Now, your father was the big, tough type. Real exciting... Know what I mean?"

"Dad was a softy, and you know it. Men like Loring went out with the stone age, Mother," Dallas returned. "I just feel sorry for his poor people. I wish I could do something for them."

"Ah!" Lisa exclaimed as though she'd just found a gold mine. "Maybe you can. Spend some time with this—"

"Sam person," Dallas provided without enthusiasm. Somehow she just couldn't see herself trying to open Loring's closed mind.

"Sam," Lisa repeated in a long, wistful breath. "Now that's a real man's name. I like the sound of it."

"I wouldn't spend time with that bully if he were the last man on earth—"

Lisa raised a finger and tilted her head. "Now, honey. Remember the down-trodden masses that need you. Think of it as a sacrifice for the good of mankind. We can work on the man part later."

"Mother, he thinks stress is just so much... hot air."

"Well, then. Give him a little taste. Make him see things your way. Open those rusty hinges."

"Just what are you suggesting, Mother?"

On Friday after working hours, Sam gritted his teeth and jabbed his punching bag in a quick one-two. He danced back, glad for the miniature gym next to his office. He shadow punched the bag with his taped fists, shaking sweat from his hair.

When he needed to trim real frustration, he worked out. Pendragon had been gnawing on him all week. When she hadn't returned Emily's calls, he'd taken the task upon himself. "Ms. Pendragon cannot take your call now, sir," he muttered, slamming into the swinging bag.

A trickle of sweat ran down his bare neck into his damp T-shirt. Somebody had to stop that crusading Joan of Arc before she turned profit into losses.

Sam glowered at the punching bag, lowering his head to throw a series of quick punches at it. In his time, he'd worked with some high-powered women, recognizing their potential. But Pendragon was a damned usurper. Since taking over the company, he'd built a policy that turned profits. He didn't want anyone messing with his baby. Dancing around the bag, Sam battered it with powerful blows.

There was something else about Pendragon that gnawed at him too, he admitted reluctantly. It was the soft hands and sweet-pea-fragrance part.

He'd stayed through the entire class because of her challenge. "If I had the guts for it," he repeated, shaking a drop of sweat from his hair. "I can take anything that broad can dish out."

The speaker in the gym buzzed. Emily's even tone announced, "Ms. Pendragon is here to see you. And it's five o'clock."

"What the hell—" Sam exploded, grabbing the swinging bag. He pressed his lips together. He'd been calling her for the past two days to set up an appointment, and now she waltzed in to catch him unprepared. Throwing a towel around his neck, Sam shouldered through the swinging door. Pressing his thumb down on the intercom's button, he said, "Emily, show her in. Then you can go."

"Thank you, sir," Emily returned a little too sweetly. Sam wiped his brow with the back of his arm. He knew his secretary's tone—it usually meant she had something up her sleeve.

Sam patted his damp face with the towel and leaned his hips back against the desk. He decided to keep the tape on his hands—he might need to take out more frustration after Pendragon swooped out of his offices. She could have had him in a clean business suit, but if she preferred to enter his turf, she'd have to take pot luck. Either way, he intended to take Pendragon out of the game.

"This way, Ms. Pendragon," Emily instructed as she opened the door for the younger woman. She leaned down to whisper just loud enough for Sam to hear, "We haven't fed him for hours. Be careful."

Emily smiled blithely when Sam glowered at her. "Ms. Pendragon says you've left a few messages for her and she thought she'd drop by. See you on Monday, Sam."

Dallas Pendragon, Sam mused, the perfect name for a crusader. Dressed in a maroon bulky-knit sweater and loose slacks, his antagonist slid the strap of her briefcase from her shoulder. The wind had caught her hair, Sam noted, tossing it in a softly feminine arrangement around her pink cheeks. The other thing Sam noted instantly was her soft rosy mouth. Like cool strawberries....

He was angry then. Because she'd dropped business protocol and hadn't arranged a meeting. Because he obviously couldn't stop noticing everything about her. Like the endless length of her legs.

She smiled slightly, just a fraction of a turn of her lips that caused something inside Sam's stomach to knot. Her gaze flicked down his T-shirt and sweat pants to the gym shoes. "Hello, Sam. I thought it best to deal with you face-to-face. I hope this isn't too inconvenient."

Wiping another drop of sweat from his jaw, Sam realized how few people had ever seen him like this. He'd had a taste of Pendragon's toughness and decided to cut the cream-and-sugar act. Pendragon was a pro; she could take it.

Sam paused a moment, savoring the moment. He was meeting her on equal ground. Pendragon wasn't the crying type. "Your timing is great. I was just punching the hell out of my equipment. If you'd like another round, let's set an appointment for Monday."

She flicked a thread from her sleeve leisurely, then glanced around his paneled office. "It's the holiday season, Sam. I like to clear out any problems as soon as I can...for peace and goodwill."

"Why didn't you return my calls?" he asked bluntly, studying the interesting curve of her backside as she turned to sit in a large chair facing him. Wiping sweat from his jaw, Sam scowled at her. Pendragon definitely did more for the chair than Emily's raw-boned figure.

Dallas tilted her head, the sleek hair sliding to expose a small earlobe with a diamond stud. Sam found he hadn't lost his fascination for the twinkling stone as she looked at him evenly. "Because I felt that the tone of the messages was rather brusque. Like a king summoning a servant."

"In other words, you decided to let me stew in my own juices," Sam supplied, realizing that in her place, he would have done the same thing.

She shrugged, accepting his accusation. Sam got the feeling that this woman could take anything he could dish out. And serve it back to him on a platter. "Something like that. What did you want?" she asked.

"I want to know how to get you off my back," he stated bluntly. Dallas had an air of cool disdain that set him off, challenging him. He hadn't been held at arm's length since he was a green recruit in the business world.

"Really? Have I been on your back?" Dallas returned, watching him intently.

Oh, God, Sam thought, he'd forgotten how penetrating those green eyes were...witch's eyes. "You know you're causing a hell of a problem, Dallas. Not only in my company, but in others. I lost a good worker today because of your spouting off that stress nonsense. And I'd be a fool to propose an employee job-sharing plan to the board. They'd laugh me out of the company."

"Maybe we should discuss our different ideas then," she offered as another trickle of sweat slid into Sam's damp T-shirt. "Are you uncomfortable with me, Sam? Or is it just that you're not dressed in your normal protective armor?"

Rising from the chair, Dallas caught the end of the towel that lay upon his chest. She blotted the sweat at his temples. "I've taken some time out of a busy schedule to deal with this matter, Sam," she offered gently. "But if you're uncomfortable dressed like this, I can wait. I really do want to get this thing settled tonight."

Because she had him off balance, Sam stilled beneath the soft patting motion of the towel. Then he jerked his head away. He began tugging the tape loose with his teeth.

Taking the task from him, Dallas unrolled the wide strips. Her fingers were slender and pale, tipped with short, neat nails. Against the broad strength of his own, they appeared very feminine and soft.

Standing close to her, Sam felt something he'd protected for years shift unsteadily.

He couldn't explain it. He just felt raw and very much in need of her attention.

He studied the soft turn of her cheeks, then again caught the fragrance that reminded him of his mother's backyard sweet peas. Taken aback, Sam stilled. Her hands completed the task efficiently, and he regretted the loss of her skin brushing his.

Dallas looked up at him unexpectedly, and Sam felt the jolt down to his gym shoes. "I want you to come home with me, Sam. For dinner." Her tone was equal to that of inviting him to a board meeting.

"I have plans," he returned roughly, moving away from her. She made him nervous, and he didn't know why. Near her, he felt as if he'd jogged fifteen miles and couldn't catch his breath.

"I know you don't have a family," Dallas added, watching him. "And that you usually work long hours. Of course, if you're afraid to accept my dinner invitation . . ."

Pendragon knew how to issue challenges, he decided darkly. He'd checked her out—she was a single mother. But he had to ask anyway, probing. "Does your husband know you're inviting me?"

She lifted a dark eyebrow. "If I had one, I don't think he'd mind." The air in Sam's lungs stilled. He'd damn well mind if he were her husband. "You could be taking a risk. Where I come from, men do the running," he added to cover his edgy reaction to her.

"Don't get any ideas, Sam. This is business. Think of it as a power dinner. And don't worry, there will be several other people there to protect you."

Sam didn't like the feeling that she fielded his remark too easily, as if she'd had much experience. He turned, running his fingers through his damp hair. "What's the point?"

Dallas glanced outside at the scant light and the drizzle hitting his office windows. "I want to take you into the working woman's point of view. See what it's like on the other side. Unless you're afraid you can't handle it. Your employees see you as inflexible anyway."

He didn't like being placed on the defensive, and Pendragon had a way of snagging his nerves. "I know what it's like to work and maintain a family—"

Crossing her arms over her chest, Dallas lifted a speculative eyebrow. "Uh-huh. You do it on a routine basis, of course."

She shifted on her long legs and took a verbal dive at him. "Let me tell you what I think your life is like, Sam. I see you have your own fitness program, yet you haven't extended one to your employees. You've kept it in your private realm. Underlings need fitness, too, you know. You probably have a streamlined life free from household duties, childrearing, home upkeep and so forth."

Sam shifted uneasily. He'd chosen his penthouse suite and employed a housekeeper because he didn't have the time nor the desire for a real home. In fact, he'd never had anything but cheap apartments early in his career and suites later. He'd chosen his present suite to accommodate occasional business parties; it was near his office, and Bertha had her own private, locked room in the basement garage. Battered and oil-sucking, the aged pickup was the one love of Sam's life. "My life-style isn't the problem."

"Isn't it?" Taking a deep breath, Dallas leveled the bottom line of her opinion straight at him. "The working class has to manage repairing their own houses and preparing their own food, right down to getting the groceries themselves. And that's all after work and picking up the kids from the babysitter. That's stress, Sam. The stuff heart attacks are made of."

"Everyone has to eat, Dallas. How or when they do it isn't a company problem."

Dallas's left eyebrow rose, her head tilting to one side in a gesture of skepticism. "So, of course, not having children and having your own private gym . . . and the ability to take extended vacations when you want them, completing your personal affairs with the help of a full-time secretary—you see no point in providing your employees with any of those benefits. Is that the bottom line, Sam?"

The muscles crossing his shoulders and running up his neck tightened. "You'd make a good kamikaze fighter, Pendragon," he admitted reluctantly. "But you don't know what you're talking about. I manage a full load here. I've got just as much stress as the next guy."

"Really?" Her appraising stare slid slowly down his body, then rose slowly upward to meet his eyes. "What I see is a man with one viewpoint. Are you afraid to experience the real working world, Sam?"

"Hell, I've worked since I can remember," he said too sharply, between his teeth. "I've done laundry and shopped for my food."

Dallas straightened her shoulders, and Sam forced himself not to glance at her breasts. "Of course, you're angry and defensive when confronted with the facts, Sam. Perhaps you're already too set in your ways to listen to new ideas ... but I'm asking you to try. You seem very brittle in business circumstances. I'd like to give you an inside view of another side of life ... and, of course, I'm willing to listen to yours. Think of it as a summit meeting.''

The thick wave of hair slid along her jaw as she lifted her head, and Sam's fingers curled with the need to touch. "No, I'm not worried about the dangers of bringing home a stranger, Sam,'' she said quietly, as though sensing his next shot. "Despite the fact that you can be obstinate and overbearing, you're not a bad guy. You'll back an employee with a reasonable grievance, and last year you personally paid overdue medical expenses for an employee's child. And you never pick on anyone half your size. I checked.''

She was tossing challenges at him again, Sam decided after a moment of grinding his teeth. She had tossed one too many. "My car or yours?''

"Actually, I took the bus to work today. I was hoping you'd give me a ride. Oh, and I'll have to pick up a few groceries along the way.'' She glanced at his sweaty workout clothes. "I can wait if you want to shower. No doubt along with your private gym, you have an executive washroom?''

Sam paused just a moment before looking down at her from his superior height. "If,'' he began firmly, "we want to accomplish anything tonight, Pendragon, I suggest you give me a little space. There are limits.''

"Your limits, of course,'' she returned, unruffled. "Your game rules.''

"I play a fair game. I'll be out in a few moments.'' Walking to his washroom, Sam couldn't resist throwing out one more taunt. "By the way, this should be entertaining.''

Sam slid his Lincoln Continental through Seattle's rainslick streets. Along the way to Dallas's home, he had somehow acquired sacks of groceries and had retrieved two small children from a babysitter. He learned that Nikki was a first grader, staying after school at the sitter's.

Seated on the front seat between Dallas and himself, Nikki and Billy openly stared at him. "Big man, Mommy," Billy stated finally.

Dallas laughed, tucking the little boy against her side. Sam listened to the sound of her laughter, the humor genuine. The black-haired child nestled to her. "Sam is nice, Billy, for all his size. That's why I brought him home. Just so he could meet you."

Sam liked the low, rich sound of her voice; it was like her touch. He glanced at Nikki, seated beside him. Lifting an eyebrow, he asked, "These are the other people you mentioned, I presume."

Over Billy's head, Dallas's eyes twinkled. "Precious, aren't they?"

Nikki turned to her mother. "Mommy, did you go daddy-shopping today like Grandma said you should? Is he Billy's present?"

For just a moment, Sam experienced the definite delight of seeing Pendragon squirm. He liked that.

"Now, honey, we talked about Sam coming to dinner. He's just going to visit with us. We have some business to straighten out, okay?"

"He's awful big," Billy said, his eyes studying Sam from head to toe. "Can you carry me, Mr. Sam?"

Warmed by the little boy, Sam answered, "As long as you like."

Nikki's hand reached up to stroke Sam's cheek, and he realized he hadn't taken time to shave for the evening. He caught the scent of chocolate and fabric softener as the small hand explored his jaw then slid away.

Suddenly, he realized he hadn't been touched by a child for years. The thought nagged at him, making him aware of the family he'd wanted as a young man. But in building his career, he'd forgotten.

"You're frowning.... Children are by nature curious, Sam," Dallas explained quietly, watching his scowl with those quiet, contemplative eyes. "But if it bothers you, we can have our meeting another time without them. This isn't painful for you in any way, is it?"

"Do you have kids, Mr. Sam?" Billy interrupted as Sam slid into the designated driveway. He parked behind a dark red compact car, which reminded him of Dallas. The car was sleek and a high performer.

"Maybe he doesn't like kids," Nikki said slowly, watching him warily as her mother left the car and helped Billy out. "My friend Kathy says some grownups don't."

"I like kids, honey. I just wasn't lucky enough to have any," Sam returned, suddenly startled by what he had just said. His ex-wife hadn't wanted children, and somehow the matter of a family hadn't occurred for years. Sam felt his body tense, and he shoveled the thought back into oblivion. He'd never toyed with regrets and didn't intend to now.

Nikki eased across the seat to slide out the door. "I like Christmas."

"Sam, would you mind bringing the groceries in?" Dallas asked, probing her purse for her keys with one hand. Billy held tight to her free one, watching Sam with big, round eyes.

In the bare light, Sam could make out a small, well-kept yard with a white board fence enclosing the back. Going up the steps to the wide front porch, Sam felt the muscles running across his stomach tighten. The homey atmosphere began with the holly wreath on the front door and spread before him. He shifted the two sacks uneasily as Dallas changed into a busy dynamo, urging him into the kitchen. At the same time, she directed the children to take off their coats and put them away.

Holding the grocery sacks, Sam caught the scents of potpourri and love warming the house. He caught a drift of something long forgotten, something too painful to remember. Of forgotten wishes, rustling in his memories like dead leaves.

"Just put the sacks on the counter, Sam," she ordered, breezing by him to a bathroom just off the kitchen. "We're having stew and French bread tonight," he heard her say over the sound of running water. "On busy days, and especially on a really hectic Friday, I like to plan a slow-cooker meal."

She reentered the kitchen, tugging up her sleeves at the elbows. "Please make yourself at home, Sam."

When he hesitated, she shot him a knowing smile. "You look so stiff—take off your jacket and tie, if you want. Kick off your shoes. If you're not comfortable, my solution will never work."

Sam just caught her sweet-pea scent as she breezed by him, turning on lamps. He had the impression of a hummingbird, darting from flower to flower. "Come on, kids. I've got your bath water running," she called. "You first, Nikki!"

In the soft light of lamps and candles, Dallas's home presented a pretty picture right down to the twinkling lights on the Christmas tree and the gaily wrapped presents. Four patchwork stockings hung from a white-enameled mantle, and Sam studied them as he stripped off his coat. A mother and two children didn't add up to four Christmas stockings. He didn't like the implication of that fourth stocking. Pendragon wasn't married, but she hadn't said anything about a boyfriend. Sam found himself scowling at the patchwork stocking.

Dallas whizzed by him, her sweatsuit creating a streak of yellow. She grinned up at him as she began unpacking the groceries with quick efficiency. "It's like this every night. A steady run until almost bedtime . . . I think Nikki is almost ready. Would you mind helping Billy finish bathing? That would leave more time for us to talk."

When Sam shifted uncomfortably, she winked. "Working men and women go through this routine every night and survive. But if you don't think you can handle a six and a four-year-old, supper will just be a little late."

Sam frowned. She'd made him feel incapable of the simple task. Rolling up his shirt sleeves, he studied her closely. Dallas caught the inquiring look and returned it evenly.

"Does something about me or tonight bother you, Sam? I really don't want you to be uncomfortable."

"Everything is fine," he answered too roughly. Dallas's tone made him uneasy. Sam wasn't used to anyone genuinely being concerned about him to see to his comfort. When she used that tone, Sam had the feeling of a soft, loving hand caressing his worries away. Long ago, he'd given up any dreams about anyone caring for him. Her quiet stare was too unguarded, too patient, and it made Sam nervous as hell. She had a way of seeing too deep, down into the murky depths of his emotions. "You're tall," he said suddenly, startled by the words that seemed to just skim out of him.

Personal comments weren't his style, but neither was the Pendragon household. She had him off balance, like a masculine Alice in Wonderland. Or maybe the potpourri scent was going to his head. Whatever it was, Sam kept studying Dallas and wondering just what was going on inside himself. "You're tall, and you move fast," he said slowly.

Great, he thought, looking down into Dallas's green witch's eyes. Since when did he care about a woman's height or the way she moved?

When she licked her lips and looked away nervously, he wanted to know then just what type of man would slow her down, long enough to taste those soft, strawberry lips. The thought curled around him warmly, startling him with an image of Pendragon's white hands fluttering on his darker skin.

"I have to move fast. There is never enough time when you have a family," she returned without missing a beat. She opened the slow cooker to stir the bubbly contents with a wooden spoon. Leaning against the counter, Dallas studied the stew intently, probing it. "It's ready."

The motion brought the sweat pants tighter around her hips, and Sam felt a sensual tightening in his midsection. He rotated his suddenly taut neck muscles. If Sam ever wanted to place his hands on a woman's soft buttocks, it was now.

His palms burned with the ache to cup— He rubbed his hands together briskly, knowing that he badly needed the support of a good stiff drink.

He turned to the bathroom, already hearing the children giggle and splash.

And then Dallas reached upward, opening a cabinet. The angle of her body caught Sam broadside. Her breasts were fuller than he had thought, her stomach just gently rounded to sweep into long slender legs...Dallas Pendragon was one neatly turned piece of woman....

She smiled over her shoulder. "Is something wrong, Sam?"

"Nothing." He swallowed to cover the tightening in his throat. Hell, he'd just been without sex for so long, he rationalized. Any woman would hit him the same way.

He had to watch Pendragon, he decided moodily. She moved inside people and turned them around. Like a virus.

Hunching his shoulders, Sam entered the steamy bathroom to find an assortment of toys and two laughing children. Nikki had already had her bath and was dressed in a flannel nightgown. Apparently she'd been handing Billy his favorite toys.

Seating himself on the closed lid of the commode, Sam grabbed the bottle of bubble bath just as Billy began pouring it liberally into the water. "Don't you think that's enough, Billy?"

The small boy looked at him seriously. "Mommy says you have to use soap to get clean," he answered piously. "Are we going to adopt you like we did our kitty? Baghdad won't come in the house even when we invite him. But you could stay in my room."

Sam reached over to drain the water from the tub. "I don't think so. Your mother and I have some business to finish tonight."

Nikki placed her hand on Sam's shoulder and he shifted uncomfortably under the light touch. Since when did kids start touching him? Since when did he like it? Sam swallowed uneasily when Nikki stroked his cheek. "Mommy always wraps Billy in a nice warm towel, then dresses him in jammies."

The boy climbed out of the tub and stared expectantly up at him. "You could carry both of us, I bet, Mr. Sam. You're real big."

Sam's heart had stopped, then began beating slowly, heavily within his ribs. The two kids were getting to him, he admitted warily, as he wrapped Billy in a towel and helped him dress in pajamas. When the task was finished, his shirt was damp and the children were bounding off to their mother.

Sitting still for a moment, Sam struggled to regain his balance. Absently opening his shirt, he rubbed the hair-covered surface thoughtfully. "Must be the Christmas season, old man," he muttered, running his fingers through his hair as he emerged from the towel-scattered bathroom.

Dallas turned from ladling stew into soup bowls just as Sam entered the large kitchen. Rumpled and distracted, Sam looked utterly... attractive, she decided after mulling the thought. "I've fed Baghdad—our cat. You can meet him later," she said, reminding herself that Sam was a business experiment, not a man—in the sensual sense. Actually Baghdad, a stray gray tom who kept returning to her home, reminded her of Sam—wary of any kindness.

Sam's hair was mussed slightly, and his frown, brooding. She ran a quick appraising look down Sam's fit body from broad shoulders to narrow hips. Maybe it was just that she wasn't used to seeing a man's chest. Dark and hairy, exposed by the damp, gaping shirt, the intriguing surface caught her gaze and held it.

Or maybe she was especially vulnerable at Christmastime, she rationalized, adjusting Billy's chair closer to hers. Pushing the thought from her mind, Dallas invited Sam to sit down. "It's not filet mignon or Baked Alaska. But it's a nourishing, easy meal for a working mother," she offered, smiling.

What was he thinking? she wondered as he continued to stare at his filled bowl. Then slowly he spoke, "I haven't had homemade stew for some time."

Nikki reached up to pat his cheek, consolingly. "Mr. Sam, you have to eat everything on your plate or Mommy won't let you have chocolate cake. It's awful good, too. She puts cherries on top. With stems, so you can eat 'em like this!" She mimed popping cherries into her mouth and jerking off the stems, grinning up at him.

"I guess I'd better eat my stew then, huh?" Sam returned the grin and Dallas noted the lines on his face shifting as though he didn't smile often. Yes, he needed help, and if her plan worked, his employees would benefit as well. He was a good sport when he wanted to be, she thought as he helped with dinner cleanup.

While Dallas tossed in a load of laundry, Sam settled down with Nikki on his lap. The little girl petted Sam's jaw and though he seemed mildly uncomfortable, he allowed the affectionate gesture. Both Billy and Nikki had instigated a study of him that Dallas considered normal; they weren't often exposed to a man within their home.

Except Douglas. She flicked a glance at Sam's long legs, the neat crease of his slacks smooth over a muscular thigh. He turned slightly, and she caught a glimpse of his chest when the shirt fell away. Douglas was absolutely hairless, she'd discovered one day at the beach. In comparison to Sam, the smaller man was ... well, more academic looking, she decided loyally. To shield her thoughtful expression, Dallas reached to check the candle beneath the simmering potpourri pot.

"We're ready to go to bed now, Mr. Sam. You can help Mommy fight the bears away and tuck us in good-night." Nikki took the story book from Sam and kissed him.

Dallas almost melted as Sam's dark eyebrows jammed together fiercely, as though he'd just experienced a sudden shock. He touched the area of Nikki's kiss lightly. Oh, Dallas thought sadly as he awkwardly patted Nikki's pajama clad bottom. The poor man just wasn't used to any sort of affection. No wonder his poor employees thought of him as inflexible and uncaring. And at Christmas season, too.

Her fingers tightened on her mug of eggnog. She'd wanted Sam to experience the hustle of a working woman returning to her home, the physical and emotional demands. She couldn't possibly allow herself to soften now.

Billy hugged her neck as she carried him to bed. He whispered in her ear. "He's got no mommy and no kids. So he's ours by rights, huh? Finders keepers? Like Baghdad?"

"We'll talk about it when he's gone, okay?" she whispered back, feeling uneasy as Sam stood at the doorway, the light in the hallway outlining his tall body.

He did remind her of an orphan, his face in shadows and his hands in his pockets as he stood outside the children's bedroom. She forced the thought from her; Sam was the corporate head of a company, and a strict manager of his employees. From what she'd seen he was hard as steel inside and out. Rubbing her hands together, Dallas decided it was time to present her business package to Sam. He'd either buy it or she'd wasted her effort on him. And three helpings of stew, plus two sizeable pieces of chocolate cake.

"Did you kill all the grizzlies, Pendragon?" he asked easily, settling down on her couch. For an odd moment, Dallas contrasted the cabbage-rose upholstery pattern to Sam's stark masculinity.

Startled by the thought of Sam as a man instead of a project, she straightened her shoulders. She admitted that Sam nettled her. He seemed like such an immovable personality.

"Okay, you've been working up to presenting your plan all evening," he stated in an ominous low voice that brought the hairs on the back of her neck standing upright. His voice was deep, gravelly, with just a drop of soft Southern drawl she hadn't noticed before. She looked at him warily from beneath her lashes.

Normally his voice was clipped and demanding like a drill sergeant's. But now the tones seemed almost... sensual, riveting her stocking-covered feet to the hardwood floor as he said, "You've been explaining the plight of the working woman to me since I arrived. Get to the point, Dallas. Why did you invite me here tonight?"

Three

For the first time since she'd conceived the details of Lisa's sketchy plan, Dallas began to feel twinges of uncertainty. Looking too powerful, Sam occupied the major portion of her couch. With his arm resting along the back of her furniture, he looked mussed and well...delectable, she admitted reluctantly.

Reaching out from her past, a curl of bitterness lodged in her stomach. At twenty-nine, she'd been easy prey for T.J.'s practiced sensuality. Looking back, her romance with T.J. was more hormonal than the grand love she had thought. Now, at thirty-nine, she had decided that passion of the red-hot variety probably would not come her way. She'd settled for a good career, a warm home and had wrapped her children around her.

Dallas found her body inclining toward Sam's weight and straightened in a jerky movement. The hard-nosed businessman weighing down his end of *her* couch shouldn't have appeal. She didn't want to think about his delighted boyish expression when he ate chocolate cake. And she didn't want to think about how she had catered to T.J., falling for that same winsome masculine expression.

Uncomfortable with the direction of her thoughts, she needed something warm and comforting in her hand. "I always have a cup of tea just after putting the kids to bed. Would you like some?"

"Anything. I'm anxious to hear your proposal, Dallas. It should top off the evening perfectly. Do you want me to help?"

The idea of Sam's large body in her kitchen flattened the breath from Dallas. She'd needed some space to recover from the evening. She hadn't expected a sensual reaction to Sam when she invited him. Suddenly, Sam stretched leisurely, his hard thigh brushing hers, and something within her started clawing its way out. Her throat dried suddenly, and a funny aching tingle raced across the tips of her breasts. Dallas tramped down the urge to slide her hand across the rippling planes of that hard thigh. *Good Lord, what was wrong with her?*

A cold chill raced over her too-tight flesh. Sam was definitely not her kind of potential romantic material. In fact— she slid a sideways glance at him—concrete was not any woman's potential romantic stuff. The man lived to work— profits and gain were in his blood, not poems and flowers.

Almost leaping to her feet, Dallas walked quickly to the kitchen. "I can manage. Just make yourself comfortable." Squaring her shoulders, Dallas had the oddest feeling that Sam had touched her, a broad sweep of warm hands flowing down her backside.

Her hands shook when she prepared the tray for tea. She frowned, studying the orchid pattern of the delicate china. Nothing more than a business wall to be scaled, Sam's physical attributes shouldn't be upsetting her. People could benefit from her project. *And all she could think about was sex.*

Her past experience had not been monumental. Dallas spared a moment to look out of the window into the night, giving herself needed space. Accidentally, she caught a movement from the Deon's window next door. The new-lyweds were tangled in a passionate embrace, kissing each other as though they needed the contact more than air.

Pressing her eyelids firmly closed, Dallas forced herself to breathe quietly for a moment. Rubbing her temple, she admitted reluctantly that the sight of Sam—sweaty from his workout—had first started her lapse. She'd patted his per-spiration away with the towel, when she really wanted to—Okay. Something haywire within her wanted to tear off her sweater and press her body against his hard one.

Her head throbbed. The whole idiotic notion was one for *The Guiness Book of World Records*. Dallas Pendragon represented the contemporary business woman, not Sheena of the Jungle responding to sensual jungle drums. She willed the momentary weakness to pass and dedicated herself to organizing her presentation. The daydreams of her ap-proaching middle age could wait.

Shaking her head, Dallas ran her thumb and forefinger up and down the bridge of her nose. Loring presented an im-mense personal challenge to her. And lodged somewhere in her brain, her mother's propaganda about peignoirs and nestling in bed with an overheated male had gotten tan-gled.

She wasn't a primitive person; she never had been . . . or so T.J. had said. To her, Loring shouldn't represent the male species; he was an experiment—one of the toughest busi-nessmen in Seattle. In her research, she'd found that he led the rat pack of high-powered businessmen. Winning him over could institute new practices that could benefit thou-sands of stressed workers. . . .

Later, seated on the opposite end of the couch from Sam, Dallas wished she would have purchased a chair in lieu of her large floor pillows and the children's bean bags.

She sipped her tea, enjoying the English blend from the china cup. The small ritual mattered and eased the tension distracting her. Sam placed his empty cup and saucer on the coffee table, then leaned back to watch her.

His hand shifted on the back of the couch, and Dallas sensed, rather then saw, the powerful muscles of his forearm. She glimpsed an expensive flat wristwatch. The short black hairs covering his dark skin glistened in the candlelight.

Dallas swallowed, realizing the intimacy of the scene. She placed her cup aside, then reached to turn on a lamp.

Sam's expression seemed to shift, tempering with humor. "It is romantic, isn't it?" he asked, his deep voice laced with humor.

The oddest edge of guilt touched her; she could feel herself preparing to blush. To recover her control, Dallas gripped the arm of the couch, crushing the cabbage-rose chintz.

"That isn't what I had in mind at all, Sam. And you should know it. It's strictly business." Dallas instantly regretted not tossing off his remark. She leaned back against the opposite end of the couch and waited for her temper to settle. If he'd just stop watching her as if he were inspecting her ulterior motives.

His hard mouth lifted just slightly, mockingly. "Isn't this cozy? The kids are in bed—they want to adopt me, by the way—and finally, thee and me—"

She took a deep breath. If there was one person in whom she hadn't expected to find a humorous streak—and deep, beguiling dimples—it was Sam Loring. "What I propose may be a little difficult to comprehend at first, but just bear with me."

"I am listening, Dallas. You haven't had any problems expressing yourself up to this point. Why don't you just spell it out?"

Moistening her dry lips, Dallas was surprised to catch Sam following the motion. She swallowed, shifting back into the security of the throw pillows. She wanted to dive under them; Loring had slashing, gray, predator eyes that could spot momentary weakness instantly.

Dallas allowed herself a frown; she wasn't into trading sensual games for career gain. "I would like to place a wager with you, Sam. One that puts my reputation on the line, and I'm very serious about it. Your end of the wager isn't that difficult, just a matter of changing a life-style for a month. I'd stand to lose far more.''

Taking a deep breath and watching Sam's intent features, Dallas fleetingly noted another quality about him missing from T.J.: *Sam listened*. While he didn't like her theories, he respected her right to express them.

Uneasily dismissing her continuing comparison between Sam and T.J., Dallas forced herself to proceed, "If I lose the wager, I will personally contact your employees and explain that my theories on stress were total nonsense. That's what you want me to do, isn't it? I really believe you'll see things differently after this experiment, Sam.''

His forefinger traced the cabbage-rose design near her shoulder. ''And I have an important part in this, no doubt. What's the part about changing a life-style for a month?''

Dallas leaned forward to explain her wager. "You'll lose the wager if you cannot—repeat, cannot—follow a working woman's routine for the most hectic work month of the year—December.''

Bending to retrieve her briefcase from the floor, Dallas snapped open the latches. "I've prepared a list, and we can go over it together. So you can better understand a working woman's routine. Of course, you don't have the necessary children, so you'll have an easier time of it.''

"What's the catch? My end of the deal is a snap," he said in clipped tones.

''We'll see,'' Dallas returned mildly, thinking of how she had stayed up all night with Billy and his flu. The next day she had worked twelve hours on classes. "But just for fun, let's say you couldn't manage running a home and working. Let's say you stepped into the life of a working woman and found it to be very uncomfortable."

Ignoring his slight snort of disbelief, Dallas prepared to slide into home base. Either he'd laugh and walk out now, or she had him interested. "Not everyone is up to the challenge of taking care of themselves and budgeting, Sam,'' she added in a I-dare-you tone that caused Sam's eyes to flicker dangerously.

He nodded curtly, lifting a thick eyebrow at her. "Go right on ahead, Pendragon. You're wading through too much bull to stop now. I've been taking care of myself for a long time, but for my own amusement, I'd like to know exactly what my end of the wager would be."

Warmed by the small victory of getting him hooked, Dallas set herself the task of reeling him in. She sensed him assessing her strengths and vulnerabilities. Whatever he was, Sam had turned his entire attention to her proposal. She had the impression that before he threw any ideas in the hogwash bucket, he'd inspect its uses first.

"My theory is that you, as a manager, just have not experienced the real working world," she said quietly, noting with satisfaction that his expression had changed to that of a bulldog determined to chew through anything in his fenced yard.

Dallas delicately threw him a bone. She shrugged and smiled with bland innocence. "If you lost—by some impossibility—I'd like to work on proposals and present them to your board—"

"Everybody wants something. But you've stepped into the wrong ball game this time, Dallas. Show me the damn list," he said in a flat tone that sounded like Billy's when his toys were endangered. "You don't know anything about me or what I can handle. I can breeze through anything you can shovel out, including a "working woman's world," he repeated the phrase with a confident sneer.

Dallas didn't want to lay out her proposal to an angry man. She wanted him receptive and in good humor. "I know you like chocolate cake, Sam," she teased lightly, foraging into his bristling manner.

"Okay, so I'm a pushover for cake," he snapped, his features hardening as though he regretted giving her a fraction of himself. "And you don't think I've got the stamina to maintain a working woman's life-style. What is it, anyway? They've got dishwashers and clothes driers, blow driers and curling irons. It's convenience all the way, right down to slower cookers and prepared foods."

"You think so? Let's look at the list and then you can either wager or—" Dallas edged closer to present the list and found her shoulder inches away from his side. At odds with Sam's masculine scent, the scent of Nikki's bubble bath crept up from his shirt sleeve.

Her heartbeat accelerated to double time and she hesitated, scouting out the scents and focusing on an uneasiness within her. Biting her lip, Dallas reluctantly chalked up one for Sam. She'd always hated the heavy scents men sometimes wore. They seemed dishonest somehow.

Like T.J.... Why did Sam cause T.J. to come strolling out of the sordid past?

"... Or I'll have you inciting riots all over Seattle, right? This whole thing is beginning to look like blackmail." Sam scowled, leaning down to read the list. He squinted, then shook his head. "I can't read anything without my glasses," he explained, reaching to extract a pair of black-rimmed glasses from his coat pocket. He slid them on, taking the list from her to study it.

Dallas found herself staring at the angle of his nose beneath the no-nonsense frames. She wondered how he had broken his nose.

Why should she care how he had broken his nose? Or why he had scars on his knuckles?

Running the palm of her hand stealthily across her rumbling stomach, Dallas decided the stew had been too spicy.

Studying Sam as he read the detailed tasks, Dallas could see that he was as receptive as hardened concrete. She shoved aside the image of his dimples; they must have been a mirage. Sam slapped the paper into her hand and sat back to stare at her. "There's not a thing there that would cause me the least bit of difficulty. You might as well start contacting those employees now."

She didn't like the high-handed way he'd thrown the wager back on her side of the court. Perhaps he needed help to realize the depth of the tasks. "Well, let's go down the items one by one and perhaps you'll see things differ- ently—"

He sighed as though thoroughly bored. "Trust me. You are wasting our time."

Dallas felt her muscles tighten and her chin lift fraction- ally. She smiled, just once and without warmth. "Perhaps you really are inflexible. I understand your *Manual of Brice Employee Rules* has never been altered. That makes a pretty strong statement to me when the workplace is constantly changing and new techniques are being found every day."

She had the satisfaction of almost—but not quite—seeing Sam Loring wince. His gray eyes slashed down at her. "I wrote it. I stand by it."

"Not one change in ten years, Sam. Yet there has been research on the hazards of and ways to prevent stress," Dallas could feel him sliding, uncomfortable with her chal- lenge. His head seemed to lower into the protective bulk of his shoulders, like a fighter on the defensive.

His fingers straightened slowly, then tightened on his thigh. "Go over the damn list, then. Lady, I'm going to take you up on your offer. Maybe it will teach you about taking risks with people who know their business."

Sam's smile wasn't nice, and Dallas found herself re- turning it in kind.

"Mmm. I admire your confidence. But we'll see what happens after the month is out." She opened the list, pointing to it. "Number one. Thou shalt do all your own private business—"

"Who the hell do you think does it?" he demanded be- tween his teeth.

"Your secretary?" Dallas offered blithely. His scowl seemed to shift from anger to caution as he looked again at the list. Sam really had no idea about the life-style she pro- posed. But he would...in detail. "No secretaries doing your personal running, Sam. Or delivering your car to the me- chanic's. Somehow during your day at work and at home, you have to find time to pick up your laundry at the clean- ers. Ah, and that's another thing—nothing but dry cleaning is allowed at the cleaners. You have to do your everyday laundry yourself. That includes towels, sheets, rugs, etcetera."

He muttered a disgruntled seaman's oath. The salty terms caused her to lift her eyebrows just once. Then pushing on, Dallas saw no reason to spare him any breathing room. "Of course, you must do your own cleaning—tub, floors, making beds, disposing of trash...."

Holding up a finger, Dallas continued while Sam began to carefully study the list. "Piece of cake," he muttered beneath his breath.

"Try number four, Sam. No use of private workout facilities. You're going to have to make time to exercise away from the company. Now that is not to say you can't use home equipment. Providing you can buy it on the average working salary. I'll tabulate that after scanning your employee wages. You must stay on that budget, Sam. That will include lunches and groceries. Oh, by the way, you have to do your own shopping and cooking and driving."

Sam sat back in the couch and stared at her blankly as she rapped off more rules: "In the office, Sam, I suggest you use your breaks to conduct your personal business, like balancing checkbooks and so forth. And remember, under no condition is your secretary to help you. She can't even straighten your desk. Nor do your Christmas shopping."

Pausing, she turned to him. Sam leveled a you-must-be-crazy look at her. Poor thing, he was just beginning to get the picture.

Because Dallas was basically sympathetic to his plight, she smiled. Then without a thought of the consequences, she reached to touch the back of his hand. "It's not a lot to ask, Sam...remember, I'm betting my reputation. For a professional to retract ideas is more dangerous than rearranging a life-style for a month."

Sam felt the soft brush of her fingers on his skin. Wading through the reality of her proposal, he realized one thing at the moment: he ached for her touch, hating the moment when her hand left him.

Taking his glasses off to place them on the coffee table, Sam settled back into the upholstery to consider the entire picture. An expert at taking problems apart, Sam weighed the advantages against the minuses. Confident about winning the wager, he itemized the other pluses of playing along.

Studying Dallas's eyes, he wondered about their shade after lovemaking. Studying the turn of her mouth, he considered its taste.

His gaze slid down the slight curve of her breasts to her legs. Sam realized he had been challenged on another level. He'd always liked an intelligent woman and he missed the sensual excitement stirring him now. Unless he was mistaken, Dallas could be a passionate woman—one to linger over, like a fine wine. He smiled slowly, savoring the moment, his excitement growing as he considered the possibilities.

Pendragon needed to pay for her troublemaking, he decided absently. But more than that, he wanted to feel the soft, lithe movement of her body beneath his.

Dallas Pendragon would share his bed—if only for a time. They were both adults; they could handle the situation when it ended. He slipped his hand lower, finding the firm curve of her shoulder. Sam liked the sleek ripple of muscle beneath his palm, like a cat being petted.

Pendragon—the woman—challenged him, made him want to hear her purr.

"I'd like to take you up on your offer, Pendragon, but I want to up the ante," he said, noting how she shifted slightly from him. He liked that—she wasn't using her femininity to add leverage to the deal. Skimming the light spray of freckles across her nose, he surveyed the corner of her mouth. It looked quite tasty. Like sweet Southern pecan pie.

The tip of Dallas's tongue flicked across her bottom lip. Sam felt his adrenaline level rise. She might be successful in business, but somehow he sensed that as a woman, Pendragon was very guarded in her relationships.

There was just something old-fashioned and very feminine about her, an element he would explore when he slipped aside her business suit and practical pumps. He allowed himself a genuine smile and added, "We're playing for big stakes here, Pendragon. It's a matter of business ethics. I don't want you to think I'm easy."

She rubbed the palm of her hand up and down her thigh briskly. For a time, Sam contented himself by studying the nervous movement. Unless he missed his bet, Pendragon had thighs like silk.

Watching her, Sam grinned at a thought skimming through him. As a boy in Georgia, he'd frolicked in a patch of sweet peas, warmed by the sun and caressed by the breeze. He had the feeling that Dallas could make him feel the same way. For a time. In his experience, good things never lasted.

Dallas faced him warily. "What do you have in mind?"

Funny, she thought, as his grin widened and the dimples crept out to full power. She hadn't thought Sam Loring would play games. But just now, he had the look of a Cheshire cat—with a mouse between his paws.

She didn't trust him. His look said he knew all about something she hadn't yet glimpsed.

His hand had somehow found her nape, his thumb caressing the length of her neck. She shivered instinctively; Sam's gray eyes darkened.

Something had shifted between them, and Dallas felt herself skidding along like a cat on ice. "Just what did you have in mind?"

He chuckled, and the sound went skittering through her— a low, sensual, barroom, know-it-all, male tone. Lifting her chin away from his stroking thumb, Dallas questioned the wisdom of inviting him to her house.

Glancing around the warmth of her home, he looked back at her. "Nice home, Dallas. Comes complete with Christmas spirit . . . kids and everything. I live in a penthouse with a housekeeper provided in the lease. I couldn't possibly manage its upkeep on a worker's salary."

"Uh-huh." She nodded slowly, watching his dimples creep into his cheeks. She felt as if she were walking on a circus tight rope, and her safety net below had huge holes in it.

Tilting his head to one side, Sam eased his left eyebrow upward. It was a scarred eyebrow; a gray hair refused to follow the line. Dallas wanted to trace her fingertip across it, smoothing it gently. But instead, she prodded, "Go ahead. I'm listening."

He sighed, stretching back against the upholstery. Lifting his arms behind his head, Sam yawned hugely. His legs stretched out endlessly and he crossed them at the ankle. "I'm going to have to work out the details."

Running his finger between his eyebrows, Sam studied the shine on his expensive dress shoes. "It's just a rough idea . . . but it goes something like this—I'm not one to overlook an opportunity to better production by new employee practices."

Frowning, he looked at her. "In the month while I'm paying my working-woman dues, I want you to make a list of the basic changes you think will benefit Brice employees. Then you and only you work up feasibility studies—costs, personnel, practices—whatever. If you can lay out a workable program—working with me—and I lose the wager, Brice will go for it. I'll back you before the board."

He shot her a perceptive glance beneath his eyebrows. "I can influence other businesses, Dallas . . . so it would be to your benefit to indulge my small adjustments to your ideas. For the sake of a better wager."

Reeling from the force of his offer, Dallas met his stare evenly. In her experience, the things that were too good to be true usually had big problems. Loring had a reputation for being a shrewd businessman. He wouldn't make that sizeable offer without catches. "And?" she probed slowly.

Rotating his shoulder against the cushions, Sam yawned again. He kicked off his shoes and studied the four Christmas stockings on the mantle. She waited as his gaze strolled across the gaily decorated tree. She had the sinking feeling Sam's big deal had a bigger catch. "Sam?"

"Uh-huh?" He turned lazily to her, the long lashes throwing spiky shadows down his lean cheeks.

Why stop now? Dallas wondered. Brice Cleansers would be a prize trophy—if only she didn't have this sinking feeling.... "Sam, I realize you're just creating ideas on the spur of the moment and I know it's rough to catch all the fine points. But let's have the major details. Now."

Sam's seemingly drowsy eyes lingered on her legs, then swept slowly upward to her face. "Well, there is just one little thing—*me*. To really give your experiment its full potential, I'd need to feel every element of stress in the average worker's life. Like children. And I couldn't possibly get the real feeling of home life at my place. Too big. I couldn't possibly support the electricity bills on an average pay. And I don't want to fire my once-a-week cook. She's elderly and knows how to make bagels."

"You're hedging, Sam. I think we've gone far enough into the discussion to lay all the cards on the table."

Nodding almost absently, Sam studied her mouth as though he found it tempting.

Dallas shifted uncomfortably, feeling her insides flutter. Sam was up to the proverbial no-good.

"Well," he said, leaning his head back against the cushions and looking at her with drowsy eyes, "if I were to live in an average house—say something like this..."

He glanced around her home, then settled back into the cushion as though it were a snugly bed pillow.

Closing his eyes, Sam sighed. "I'd really like to spend my month of hardships here, Dallas. With you. You can keep an eye on me that way... see that I don't cheat."

Dallas dropped through the imaginary tight rope's safety net. For a moment she couldn't breathe. Living with a man was an experience she did not want to repeat. T.J. had watched television while she had struggled frantically with laundry, cleaning and managing insufficient-funds notices.

Sam couldn't possibly manage two children—

As she did frequently when upset, Dallas thought she could devour two boxes of cherry-covered chocolates. "Sam, you're tired. We'll have lunch tomorrow and discuss a more reasonable plan, okay?"

"Afraid?" The soft Southern drawl had returned, his eyes opening slowly to flicker over her face.

"Not on your life, Loring," she managed unsteadily after a moment.

"I'm housebroken. I'll make my bed and work out expenses with you. I'll do all the laundry and baby-sit like a live-in nanny anytime you want. What's more, I can experience the entire picture." He shrugged slowly. "Of course, it's up to you."

"No way..." Dallas said slowly in a low voice. "Look, Sam. Admit it. You can't cut it and you're looking for ways out—"

Suddenly, the drowsy eyes were replaced by a sharp, predatory gleam. "Oh, can't I? Lady, I can handle anything you can dish out."

While Dallas dealt with the new angles on her wager, Sam pulled out his dimples. "Come on, Pendragon. I'll be disappointed if you back out now...just because *you* couldn't cut it."

His thumb warmed a path down the side of her neck. Dallas forced herself to hold still as she took his wrist between her thumb and forefinger. Beneath her light grasp, his pulse was pounding as rapidly as hers. The thought that Sam was responding to her—excited by her—sent a series of shockwaves through her.

She swallowed the dry wad that seemed to be lodged in her throat. Sam, sitting with his shirt agape, his chest textured with a dark covering of hair, was too...stimulating. "No, Sam," she whispered unevenly. "How would I explain...?"

"You'll think of something," he answered quietly, soothingly. "I trust you."

Could she trust herself?

"No, Sam," she whispered weakly. She was either hearing her own heartbeat...or those damned jungle tom-toms.

"It's for the good of everyone," he insisted in that musical Southern drawl. But Dallas found she couldn't look away from that dark, hairy wedge exposed by his shirt. On her thigh, her fingertips flexed, wanting to stroke the rough hair on his chest. She swallowed, suddenly realizing how very much she wanted to nuzzle—

Forcing herself to look upward, Dallas found Sam watching her quietly. The hard gray eyes had darkened, the shadows of the room flickering about him. Taking her hand, Sam placed it upon his chest, holding it gently with his own. The rough hair shifted and tickled her palm, and Dallas's eyes involuntarily drifted down to their hands.

His heart beat slowly, heavily beneath her touch. Like a sleeping beast waiting to be awakened. The feelings she had about him during the biorhythm experiment came rushing back: his loneliness reached out to her. And she responded.

His fingers slid down to her wrist, raising it to his mouth. For a moment, his breath hovered against skin. Then holding her gaze, Sam put his lips in the center of her palm. Watching her, he waited, the hard lips warming her flesh without asking. Poor Sam, she thought, bemused by the sensations washing over her. He's so alone. He's aching—

Then his lips moved against her flesh, nibbling the sensitive pads. Dallas shivered, feeling a wave of heat beat against her.

Placing her hand along his jaw, Sam began to breathe unevenly. Then he trembled, making her aware of his vulnerability. Taking his time, Sam traced the shape of her mouth with his finger. "Don't be afraid," he whispered huskily.

Dallas couldn't move, savoring the warm path of his hand across her face. She saw him closing out the room, leaning toward her.

And then his mouth touched hers. The sweet, delicate brush of lips tasting, moving—

"Oh, Sam," she heard herself sigh as the touch went on, wooing, teasing, tormenting. Closing her eyelids, Dallas allowed herself to fall beneath his gentleness.

She hadn't expected that—the gentle, caring touch—she realized distantly. Somehow she hadn't thought about Sam that way at all. He cherished, she decided as she allowed his mouth to trace a path to her ear.

Resting against her cheek, he breathed slowly, the warmth swirling around her. "Come here, sweet pea," he whispered, gently drawing her into his arms.

Four

———

At eight o'clock on Saturday morning, Dallas lay dozing and tangled in her rosebud-patterned sheets. She tried to ignore the hushed, happy noises coming from her living room. She needed her rest to cope with Sam's new twist on her wager.

Turning over to her stomach, she covered her head with a pillow, muffling the children's excited tones. Sam's sweet kiss had destroyed a good night's sleep, filling her with doubts she didn't want explored.

For a woman who had decided romance had passed her over, Dallas recognized the disturbing signals created by the kiss. If Loring kissed her as though she was soft, feminine and much more delicate than her five foot, nine inches, it was because he was planning an ambush. Frowning and stretching her legs, Dallas groaned.

Sam wasn't anything but trouble. According to his employees, workaholic Sam Loring did not possess a smattering of sensitivity.

Groaning again, Dallas knew she should keep Loring at a distance. His style could only be compared with a Sherman tank. A man his size was easy to see coming. She remembered how devastatingly male he had appeared in his workout suit. When she had touched him in the stress class, sensing him through her fingertips, she could feel the raw power simmering beneath his taut muscles.

She turned onto her side, holding the pillow over her ears and watching the stormy skies over Seattle through her lacy curtains. She closed her eyes and wondered why that single, tender kiss had devastated her.

She barely remembered T.J.'s kisses, and Douglas's pecks had reminded her of Billy's. But Sam's reached straight into the aching heart of her.

Scowling, Dallas labeled Sam as an ambusher with his sights set on invading her privacy just for sheer orneriness.

Dallas groaned aloud, kicking free of her tangled sheets. She unbuttoned her nightgown's high, frilly eyelet collar and pressed her fingers to her throat, thinking how her pulse had throbbed quietly after the kiss.

What nonsense, she groused, flopping onto her back. Here she was, a divorcée, sliding out of youth's idealistic bloom with two children in tow. Just last night—before the wager and the kiss—she had been headed for a comfortable middle-age and building a satisfying, profitable career. She didn't need Loring messing up her household or her life. True, he was a sizeable stumbling block, but she could cut him down to size.

Beat Sam Loring? she asked, thinking of his furious expression during the class and in his office. Savagery ran just beneath his expensive, well-groomed exterior. He handled his business affairs like a shark scenting blood, and she wanted to keep him out of her personal waters.

Dallas bit her lip, pushing down an uneasy premonition that Sam believed in an eye for an eye—she had invaded his territory, therefore he had squatter's rights on her home.

She frowned, scowling again at the gray skies. Loring was deceptive. He moved too fast for a big man and pulled out dimples and a Southern drawl on a whim. And last night, he even had the nerve to invite himself over for morning coffee.

If she hadn't been so dazed by that insidious, hateful, sweet kiss, she would have thrown him out on his ear.

In the living room, Billy let out a delighted shriek, and Dallas sighed. She caught the scent of coffee and jumped to her feet. The last time Nikki attempted to make coffee, the kitchen took an hour to clean. "I'm awake now," she teased in a loud, ominous tone as she walked toward the living room in a swirl of ankle-length, rosebud-flecked nightgown.

The sight of Sam Loring sprawled on his stomach over her carpeting, dressed in a navy-blue sweatshirt and worn jeans, stopped her in the doorway. Spread before Sam was the beginnings of a doll house, and Nikki was holding the directions up for him to read. Dressed in his pajamas, Billy lay down the length of Sam's broad back, examining the handiwork from over Sam's broad shoulder. Clutched in Billy's small hand was a shining new dump truck.

Baghdad, who had apparently felt safe entering the house with another grown male nearby, rubbed against Dallas's legs.

Nikki looked up at her mother and glowed, looking picture-adorable in her ruffly flannel nightgown. "He gave me a doll house, and then maybe this afternoon—or when you say it's okay—we're going shopping for furniture. He knows the Sunbird Girls' Group smile song. And he'll buy all the Sunbird Sunny Sugar Cookies I can carry at one time. Billy got a truck, and Sam's going to make him a sandpile to play in—if you say it's okay," she qualified with a grin.

"Oh no," Sam heard Dallas whisper as he turned his head to follow Nikki's wide grin.

Standing in the muted light of the hallway, Dallas closed her eyes as though willing him away into heavy Seattle traffic. Her fists pressed against the folds of her gown, and

Sam found himself mentally stripping it from her to find the warm, soft welcoming flesh beneath.

Sam had spent an uneasy night sorting out the kiss he had given Dallas and the sweet, shy way she had responded. Resting pliantly in his arms later, Dallas's changing expressions had fascinated Sam. She had been surprised to find her fingers prowling through the hair on his chest, looking at her hand as though it were a disconnected probe. Dallas Pendragon, despite her career-woman exterior, was unjaded, untasted and highly desirable. That kiss had cost Sam two cold showers during the night. While Dallas wanted to undermine his kingdom, keeping business cold and above the heat of passion, Sam's inclinations ran more to seducing her.

The light behind her outlined long legs and gently curving hips beneath her gown. With a high neck and puffy sleeves that ended at her wrists, the modest gown was the sexiest thing Sam had experienced in years. It gave him the feeling of waiting for his Christmas package to be unwrapped layer by layer. The women in his past wore lace negligees and teddies designed to promote the response that Dallas's prim gown was so thoroughly doing.

Sam shifted uncomfortably. If ever he had wanted to carry a woman back to bed and linger throughout a lazy weekend, it was now. He'd ignored a potential virus before, but suddenly her ability to raise his temperature was appealing.

The thought startled him. In his lifetime, Sam had never lingered overlong with any bedmate. "I'm still here," Sam stated quietly, watching her.

He remembered the warm, silky feel of her hair sliding through his fingers. Now the sleek strands swirled about her face as she shook her head as if to clear it. "What are you doing here this early?"

With the morning light outlining her body, and her mouth tight with displeasure, Dallas was beautiful. Grinning and thoroughly enjoying the moment, Sam wanted to sweep her into his lap and kiss her awake. "I get up early," he said,

watching her scowl at the nearly-completed dollhouse and
the truck Billy clutched tightly to him.

"And I like privacy on Saturday mornings," she stated
bluntly, running her fingers through her hair with the distracted air of one who has just crossed time warps.

"I'll remember that." Not taking his gaze from her, Sam
shifted to a sitting position, pulling Billy, blanket and truck
into his lap at the same time. Nikki knelt beside him, drap-
ing her arm around his neck.

Surrounded by the scent and warmth of the children, the
colorful trappings of Christmas and a grumpy, displaced
Dallas, Sam was totally happy.

The thought was disquieting. He hadn't relaxed for so
long that it made him uneasy, but he pushed the feeling aside
to watch Dallas's determined struggle for control.

Dallas swallowed, frowned and ordered quietly, "Nikki,
Billy... go... feed the cat."

Nikki whispered loudly in Sam's ear, "See? She's not
happy on Saturday mornings if we wake her up. Come on,
Billy. Mommy's got *the look*."

Billy cast a wistful glance over his shoulder, but allowed
himself to be drawn after Nikki into the kitchen. Immediately after the children left the room, Dallas hissed, "Go
away, Sam. Shoo. Don't call me. I'll call you."

Rising carefully to avoid the scattered pieces of the doll
house, Sam found himself walking toward Dallas. Looking
confused and flushed and warm from her bed, she needed
tormenting. Any woman who had caused him time and effort wondering how to take her out gently—dispensing with
her meddling in his business—*and* explore her sensually was
trouble. He was vaguely angry at himself for being tempted,
and so he leered down at her. "I haven't been shooed away
in years, sweet pea."

"Scat!" she added venomously as she took a step back,
flicking her hand at him as though he were a worrisome
puppy. When Sam stopped in front of her, she glared up at
him sulkily and crossed her arms over her chest. "I'm not
up to you this morning."

"Have your coffee. You'll feel better," he offered solicitously, feeling the soft heat of her cheek as he brushed aside a silky strand of her hair. He wondered suddenly what other men had seen her dressed so cuddly and sexy and felt himself go raw. When he had her in his bed, he'd wipe out any other players.

She jerked away from his light touch, breathing unevenly. Sam liked watching her flounder through waking up to his presence; he had a quick flash of what it would be to wake up beside her, to nuzzle that sweet spot just below the ear. Dallas, he sensed, was virtually untutored in waking up to a lover's demands. Now she threw up her hands. "You're too big, take up too much space, and I don't want you here. Scat," she repeated darkly.

"I could move in this afternoon and we can be practically right on schedule with the wager by Monday," he offered softly, watching her soft mouth part in surprise. A sudden gush of elation soared unaccountably to Sam's head, and if he were truthful, his body was reacting sensually to her nearness. When he gave in to an impulse and touched the rapidly pulsing vein in her throat, she swatted at him, and Sam caught her hand. Dallas obviously wasn't accustomed to being touched or kissed by a man. The angry color rose in her cheeks as he said, "You can tell the kids you're adopting me for a month—"

A key turned in the lock and the door swung open to reveal a small, sixtyish blond woman dressed in a pearl-studded gray sweater and matching pants. Her surprised expression changed when she scanned Dallas's nightgown and blush. Lazily, the woman's gaze drifted down Sam's fit backside, her mouth curving slowly, knowingly into a smile. "Well, well," she stated in a tone that said she had assessed the situation and had come to her own conclusions.

"He's not mine," Dallas stated flatly, jerking her hand away from Sam. "He's just getting ready to leave."

"Whose is he?" asked the woman, crossing over to him. "My dear, I didn't know you would actually take my advice and bring home a real live man—"

"Mother," Dallas said between her teeth, rubbing her wrist as though to rid herself of his touch. "This is Sam Loring. Sam... my mother, Lisa."

"Charmed," Lisa returned, her speculative gaze drifting between her daughter and Sam. "Married, are you, Sam?"

He liked Lisa immediately, recognizing her as a player. Sam lifted her hand to kiss it. "I'm available," he answered, grinning.

"Children?" Lisa cooed, flicking an oh-my-you'd-better-catch-this-one expression at Dallas.

Sam recognized the look and glanced down at Dallas, who was glaring at them both. "I'm hoping your daughter will loan me hers," he answered softly. "I'm going to be staying here, you know. We're setting up housekeeping and we'll be working together. A pilot project—"

"A pilot project at work—not here," Dallas interrupted.

"*Here* would be a first for me," Sam responded silkily.

"Don't hand me that—you're old enough to have lived through several situations just like this one," Dallas shot back hotly.

"Never... quite like this," Sam emphasized, his eyes sparkling.

Lisa's eyes widened, then the woman gave her daughter a brilliant, pleased smile. "Oh, my," she said in an ecstatic sigh.

"Oh...rats," Dallas hissed before throwing up her hands and stomping off to her room.

Lisa patted Sam's shoulder, tested the heavy muscles in a series of light probes, then slowly walked around him, eyeing him up and down. "My, you are a big one...." Lisa waved a dismissing hand in her daughter's direction, lowering her voice. "She hasn't had her coffee. Don't say anything until she has had at least two cups.... You have definite potential, you know. She usually picks wimps."

Sam grinned, recognizing a would-be partner in crime. "Ma'am, I'd be proud if you'd have coffee with the family and me. I brought fresh-baked bagels," he offered in his deepest Southern drawl.

"My, my, I do declare," Lisa exclaimed softly as Sam began to prepare the children's favorite cereal and poured her coffee. Without missing a beat, he stopped a threatening skirmish between the children by picking each one up, tossing them lightly in the air and catching them in a hug until they giggled and settled down to eating.

"Mother? Could I see you . . . *now*?" Dallas called ominously from her bedroom.

"I'm being summoned," Lisa whispered in the tone of a conspirator, then poured a cup of coffee for her daughter. "You won't go away until we can chat more, will you, Sam?"

Sam found a carafe and filled it with coffee, then placed it on a tray with Dallas's and Lisa's filled cups. Studying the effect, he toasted a bagel, buttered it and added it to the tray. "Tell her she can come out when she's feeling better, will you? I intend to spend the day with her and the kids. . . ."

"It's nice here, isn't it, Sam?" Lisa asked knowingly, slanting a look up at him.

He nodded curtly, realizing suddenly how excited he had been throughout the long night, just waiting for morning. Dallas's rumpled, disgruntled ornery self hadn't disappointed him. While he intended to enjoy her, his game plan called for getting the controlling hand.

He met Lisa's assessing gaze unflinchingly, and the look held. "This should be quite interesting," she murmured quietly.

"Quite," he repeated smiling.

"Be gentle, dear . . . it's my duty as a mother to say that. But Dallas can be such a beast if you cross her. I'll send you flowers if you recover," Lisa advised, picking up the breakfast tray. She carried it into the beast's lair.

In her bedroom, Dallas was busily stripping off her nightgown and jerking on jeans and a sweatshirt. She glared at Lisa when the woman entered the feminine room and placed the tray on an antique oak dresser. Lisa's expression was too innocent. "Don't get any big ideas, Mother."

"Who, me?"

"He's business. He's the manager I was telling you about—the workaholic who needs to experience the working woman's world?"

"He's lovely. Has a raw sexual magnetism, dimples and a lovely Southern drawl—and all that genuine masculine charm. Of course, I don't have any big ideas," Lisa stated, handing Dallas her coffee. "He's just your typical run-of-the-mill wimp," she concluded airily, sipping from her cup.

"He wants to live here and experience *your* plan in my home, with my children," Dallas stated darkly, eyeing her mother as she sat on the four-poster bed's pink-and-mauve patchwork quilt. Lisa fussed with the assortment of throw pillows and studied the rosebuds, and Dallas didn't trust her a bit. "Don't encourage him."

"Oh, I wouldn't ever do that, dear," Lisa responded wryly. "Now, just what is the scam?"

Dallas glanced at the closed door, then lowered her voice in hushed tones. "It's your fault. When I proposed *your* plan to him, he started throwing in conditions. He wants to live here—with us. The whole thing is impossible. He just appeared in my living room this morning. He's bribed Nikki and Billy and he's *out there in my kitchen*."

Dallas could feel the panic in her voice streaking through her. *Sweet pea* he had said, placing his mouth ever so carefully over hers. Somehow she had found herself sinking into that gentle kiss, warming to the security it offered. The thought was ridiculous, considering Sam Loring was out to get her. "He's just too big, too aggressive," she said firmly. "I don't like him."

"I think he's sweet. Why don't you try the bagel he buttered for you?"

Dallas stared at the bagel as though it were a live, venomous snake.

"He's quite domestic, Dallas dear—"

"You don't have any idea what sort of man he is," Dallas stated carefully. "Live with us," she repeated, thinking through exactly what that could mean. She had pampered T.J. until she was exhausted, and she never wanted to repeat the experience again. For his size, Loring would eat twice as much, be twice as sloppy, use more hot water when he showered ... Dallas forced her negative projections to stop. She didn't want to think of Sam sleeping and taking showers under her roof.

"You took in Baghdad, didn't you?" Lisa shrugged, lifting her expressive eyebrows. "How bad do you want it?"

Caught unaware with the image of Sam's water-beaded body behind her eyelids, Dallas reddened instantly and turned angrily on her mother. "Want what?"

"Why, the miraculous cure for the working women you're fighting so hard for, dear," Lisa returned innocently. "What else could you possibly want?"

"He can't make it," Dallas stated firmly.

"Make what?"

"Mother! Sam Loring is not an average suburbanite. He's a business czar delegating his needs to others."

"Well, then. He's bound to lose the bet, isn't he?" Lisa interrupted smoothly. "He couldn't possibly do all the mundane things working women have to do, could he? Why are you so worried?"

"Why am I worried?" Dallas repeated warily as she entered her small kitchen to see Sam sprawled over a chair, reading the morning paper and drinking his coffee. She glared at his expensive, comfortable joggers which occupied two large linoleum squares. He was encroaching on her life and her precious Saturday morning, and she wanted him gone.

"What have you done with my children?" she demanded, discarding the way she had planned to tactfully remove him from her home.

He rattled the sports page, his head sinking lower into the paper. "They're getting dressed. The Seahawks are in great shape, aren't they?" he asked, referring to Seattle's football team.

When she didn't answer, he glanced up at her. "Something wrong?"

"Why are you here?" Inwardly, Dallas promised to pay her mother back for suggesting this insane idea.

"We have to make plans to move me in this weekend—"

"I'm leaving," Lisa called from the living room. "Nice meeting you, Sam."

"Come back soon," he returned as though he already were a resident in good standing. Uncoiling himself from the chair, Sam cleared the breakfast dishes, rinsed and placed them in the dishwasher, then sponged off the vinyl tablecloth. "The kids will be ready to go just as soon as you are. Nikki needs some furniture for her dollhouse, and we could use the outing to introduce the idea of me moving in."

"Moving in?" Dallas repeated dully, a quiver of fear beginning low in her stomach. She hadn't shared any part of her daily routine with a man since T.J. Her life was perfectly well ordered and liveable, and suited her totally.

He trailed a finger down the side of her throat. "I can't see any reason not to start as soon as possible. I'll leave it up to you what to tell the kids. But I suggest the adoption method as long as they know it's just for the holiday season. They already feel sorry for me because no one's hung a stocking for me . . . they think I'm deprived."

"Kind of you to offer suggestions." Dallas stepped away from that warm finger. "I haven't decided to accept your conditions yet. You just may have to stay in your pitiful penthouse and manage the best you can."

"It's lonely," he said quietly behind her.

Double Drat! Dallas thought warily as she remembered her sympathetic reaction to his loneliness in class. Ambushers typically pulled out unexpected weapons, and she could feel her heartstrings twang unaccountably. She couldn't afford to spend any sympathy on Loring, he'd use it against her. She could feel his warmth seeping through her clothes.

"Don't you want me to experience real stress? Kids? Upkeep? You're not frightened of me, are you, Dallas?"

The soft Southern taunt inflamed her. She turned slowly, looking up at his quiet, pensive expression. "Not on your best day, Loring. You haven't got anything that could possibly make me back down."

"Oh, haven't I?" he asked, his dimples appearing as he grinned. She noted the places and lines shifting within his dark skin. When he smiled, oozing charm, he could be dangerous.

"No," she answered huskily, then wondered if he really did have something that could make her—

Distracted momentarily, her thoughts went back to yesterday afternoon when she'd surprised him in his boxing workout. Looking sweaty, virile and totally sexy, Sam definitely possessed the right equipment.... But for some other woman, one without a mission.

"I can move in tonight, if the children are agreeable. That will give us all day tomorrow to work on budgets and routines. What are you telling the children?"

"We go to church on Sundays," she said, gloating that she had foiled his plans for encroaching.

He shrugged, grinning. "Fine. We can spend this afternoon plotting."

Forcing herself to breathe quietly despite her rising anger, Dallas eyed him menacingly. It was difficult to menace when a six-foot-four, very fit man with dimples was grinning down at her. Only the thought of how she could make him squirm at the office kept her from throwing him out into the gray Christmas-season day. "I'll work on it," she said between her teeth. "Okay, the deal is on. You can move in. But if you step out of line just once, you're out of here, Loring."

"I love it when you get tough, Pendragon. Where are you putting me?"

Dallas knew where she'd like to put him. But in lieu of cramming him into a mailing carton, she settled for a necessary conversation with her children. Sam discreetly vanished into the kitchen while the children and Dallas sat down for a couch conference. Nikki quickly understood that Sam would visit for a month, then return to his own home, rather like her friends did after her slumber parties. But Billy wanted to adopt Sam. "He's ours," the little boy argued.

Dallas took a deep breath and replied just as firmly that Sam could be borrowed, but had to be returned after a month, just like Billy's favorite library books.

When both children completely understood and agreed to the situation, Dallas took another deep breath. She turned to find Sam grinning at her from the kitchen. "Okay," she said without explanation, then watched his I'm-in grin widen.

By that evening, Sam had installed his larger bed in Dallas's guest bedroom. They had gone shopping for doll furniture and a smaller truck for Billy, although Sam had mentioned rather wistfully that he had always wanted a toy train set. Sam could be beguiling, Dallas noted reluctantly. She'd have to watch the way he appealed to her soft spots, because she intended to give him hell for wrecking her Saturday morning.

Dallas had reluctantly allowed Sam's longer, wider bed. "Don't get the idea you can move in anything without my permission," Dallas had sniffed when he finished stowing her four-poster guest bed in the basement. "The neighbors are going to talk as it is. Your junkyard pickup isn't helping the picture."

Sam had really taken offense at that remark—Bertha had seen better days. A vintage Ford, she'd crossed the United States with him. He loved her, and where he went, Bertha would be parked.

"I'll make friends with the neighbors," he had stated too quietly. "If the Lincoln was parked in your driveway instead of Bertha, they might think I'm keeping you," he added smugly, watching her absorb the taunt.

Dallas had settled for slamming pots and pans around in the kitchen, and when he had asked if he could help her, she had glared at him. Sam retreated into the living room to watch cartoons with the children, who immediately dived on top of him for a brief tussle.

After dinner, Sam began clearing away the table. He worked with Dallas, who continued to shoot dark, threatening glances his way. "Something wrong?" he asked innocently as the dishwasher began first to hum, then changed to thumping noises.

She kicked it, pumped hand cream into her palms and rubbed them together briskly. "I don't have time to deal with you tonight, Loring. I've got a date, and Mother will be coming over to babysit. Just stay out of everyone's way until we can hash this out, will you?"

Something dark and ugly moved within Sam, something he hadn't felt for years, back when he made extra money by performing bare-knuckle fights in back alleys. "A date? With who?" he asked darkly, before he realized he had spoken. It hadn't occurred to him that Dallas would have a boyfriend or fiancé; her kiss had been too untutored.

She nodded, smiling sweetly. "Mmm. I have dates, you know. Just try not to make yourself too obvious until we work this whole thing out. You will have to keep your... women away from my home. And that's a ground rule. Don't tie up my phone with them, either," she added after a moment's thought.

"As you wish, my dear," he murmured, watching her wary expression. He'd moved corporations aside neatly in business, he wasn't about to let a wimp—as Lisa described Dallas's romantic interests—push him around. "I'll have to satisfy elsewhere," he drawled.

"I hope they aren't costly," she returned sweetly. "You'll be on a budget, you know." With that, she sauntered off to prepare for her date.

When Dallas entered the livingroom, she found Sam sitting at one end of the cabbage-rose couch, with Nikki and Billy seated on his lap. Beau Michaelson occupied the other end uneasily as the trio examined him as though he were about to commit a crime. Disney cartoons played happily across the television set as Sam asked quietly, "So, what do you do for a living, Beau?"

Spying Dallas, Beau rose to his feet, obviously relieved.

"Your mother can't babysit. She has a hot date," Sam seemed to growl. He took in the special care she had taken preparing for her date. His long, assessing look started its way at the top of her freshly shampooed and curled ringlets to the slight brush of cosmetics on her flushed skin.

The look lingered and held as it slid down the neat, basic-black sheath fitting her body closely. Just because she was in a rebellious mood, Dallas had added her favorite nylons—black silk with seams and embossed bows at the back of her ankles—and Sam slowly, inch by inch, took in every curve down her high, stylish heels. "Well, well," he said slowly, his eyes gleaming behind the glasses as they met hers. "Naughty, but nice."

"We'd better go," Beau muttered, stepping around Sam gingerly to place Dallas's coat on her shoulders.

"We'll be at this number, Sam." Dallas jotted down the theater's number and placed it by the phone. In doing so, she caught Sam's expression. His grey eyes were stormy, his tall muscular body tensed as though he wanted to beat someone. She had never seen such raw fury in a man's face, and the look bound her for a fraction of time . . . until Sam smiled nastily. He had the look of a junkyard dog baring his teeth quietly and waiting for one vulnerable moment. "Have fun, kids."

"Who is he?" Beau asked in a hiss as they walked to his car. Glancing back at the gaily Christmas-trimmed house, Dallas spotted Sam standing in her doorway and looking as though he'd been wedged into it for the duration.

He waved and called again, "Have fun."

Beau glanced uneasily at Dallas. "Who is he?" he insisted, helping her into his car.

The matter was too complicated, and Dallas closed her eyes, resting her head against the support. "One of mother's friends, down on his luck," she lied, unable to tell the truth. "I'm just helping out."

"He looks tough," Beau commented anxiously. "Are you sure he's the right kind of house guest?"

"I can handle him," Dallas answered firmly, and meant it.

After her date, Sam cheerfully greeted them on the porch. Dallas *had* intended to compare Beau's kiss to Sam's and had wasted an entire evening encouraging the shy man.

"How about a beer, Beau? Dallas always has a nice cup of tea when things settle down for the night, don't you?" he asked warmly as his gaze thoroughly inventoried Dallas's dress and unkissed mouth. His tone implied that Dallas required tea and *him* to relax her.

Beau mumbled something about rechecking statistics and almost fell down the steps, then disappeared. While Dallas glared at Sam, he raised an eyebrow. "Did I interrupt?" he asked innocently as she marched past him into the sanctity of her bedroom.

At midnight, Dallas worked to up the ante, making lists of chores for Sam to share. She arranged a daily schedule, taking extreme care with the morning bathroom roster and the evening settling-down routine. Sitting cross-legged on her bed in the midst of her notes, legal pads and pens, Dallas tried not to notice the muffled noises in the bedroom next to hers. She viciously punched her hand calculator, averaging the Brice clerical workers' salaries, then smiled grimly. In a very short time, Sam would understand the stressful realities of a Brice worker.

Finally at three o'clock in the morning, she replaced her copious lists in her briefcase and crawled under her rosebud sheets.

She sighed, listened to the quiet house and snuggled down with the air of one who had performed a task well. Poised on the brink of sleep, she thought she heard Sam say softly, "Nite-nite."

Five

"The Seahawks can wait," Dallas stated the next afternoon when they all had returned from church. Sam was sprawled before the television set, and the children were napping. "We have some sorting out to take care of, if you'll remember," she added nastily, still vexed about his "Nite-nite."

Ordinarily on a Sunday afternoon, Dallas would snuggle down on the couch, doze beneath her afghan and spend a leisurely evening with the children. But she thought of the workers depending upon her, the wager and Sam's tyrannical move into her home. She wondered briefly if it were possible to send a grown man to his room indefinitely—Sam wasn't the type to be shipped off anywhere without his consent. He was in her home to cause trouble, and she could see it coming in big, black spades.

The man was manipulative, insensitive. She glanced uneasily at his hard mouth. If Beau had just kissed her before Sam had appeared, then she could have had a comparison to that damn, nagging, sweet kiss.

She was too old to be called "sweet pea." Too seasoned to believe in the promises of a man's raspy, sexy tone. After all, T.J. had taught her a hard lesson, and she should know better.

Why had she sunk into Sam's kiss with all the resistance of a kid to candy?

Sam was going to pay for that memorable kiss.

"Sure thing. If you want to talk, we'll turn off the Seahawks," Sam agreed, snapping off the television. In a blue cotton sweater, jeans and joggers, Sam was too appealing. The loose neckline had slipped aside, allowing Dallas a glimpse of dark hair on his chest, which unaccountably unsettled her. His hair was mussed and behind his lenses, Sam's gray eyes were saying things to her about ways to spend a lazy Sunday afternoon.

Waking up to his hushed voice quieting the children as they ate breakfast, entering the bathroom scented with his after-shave and seeing the array of masculine items on her shelf had already darkened Dallas's Sunday.

She had studied the razor and shaving cream for a moment, the expensive after-shave near her toiletries. Gripping the edge of the vanity, Dallas had closed her eyes. She just didn't want to remember how she had suffered at T.J.'s hands—the denigrating residue of a woman who had been used as a provider, a mother and a bed partner.

A bed partner, she had repeated. Classified by Lisa as a "lazy, egotistical jock," T.J.'s lovemaking left Dallas's expectations at the oh-well level.

She had been a fool, trusting a man who frequently indulged in other loves. Douglas, whom she'd dated casually, was an experiment, and she had regretted coaxing him into semipassion.

Well, passion for him, she admitted. With damp, limp lips and groping hands, he had interpreted her revulsion as an innocent's shyness. After explaining to him that she simply couldn't come up to his skilled standards, Dallas ended the relationship. Relieved that he had magnanimously accepted her explanation, Dallas gifted herself with a whole box of chocolate-covered cherries. It had taken her years to draw her shell and her family safely about her, and she didn't trust Sam's sexy look this afternoon at all.

The part of her that had been so repulsed at working up a passion for Douglas wanted to simply throw herself upon Sam's fit body. Drawing her nails down the couch's cabbage roses, Dallas expected that she wouldn't have to maneuver Sam into passion; he'd already be there, hot and waiting. She also expected that with the hunger roaming unsatisfied within her, she'd be equal to the challenge. And not at all repulsed by his hard hands exploring her body.

Dallas glanced at his backside and rephrased the matter of the hands on body. Was it her soft hands exploring *his* body?

She forced her eyelids closed and concentrated on the task at hand. Sam Loring had agreed to be stuffed into the mold of a working woman. Of course, he wouldn't be able to handle it, and that single thought warmed her. She decided to reward herself with two boxes of chocolates and a pecan pie for winning the wager.

Lying still on the floor, Sam propped his head on his hand and just looked at her. "Whatever you're mulling over isn't pleasant. The sooner we settle into a routine, the better it will be for the kids, don't you think?"

Dallas eased herself down on the sofa, taking care to place as much room between her and the squatter as possible. Sam had entered her children's lives. They were hers and she didn't intend for them to become attached to her temporary resident. He wouldn't be so glib once she read her extensive lists, she thought, anticipating his outrage, his anger, his bowing out of the wager like a whipped—

Sam barely scanned the lists she thrust at him. He shrugged, his gaze strolling over her rust-colored sweatsuit. "Fine."

He glanced again at the salary she had pinpointed for his use. When a small muscle in his cheek tensed, Dallas pursed her lips to keep from smiling.

"When was the last time you lived with a man?" he asked flatly, tossing the papers to her open briefcase on the floor.

Her body tightened, responding to Sam's intense stare. "You're supposed to be thorough. You've probably already had me checked out . . . you should know."

He nodded, his hard mouth lifting in a grim smile. "Okay, I know," he said softly.

When she looked at him closely, wondering what he actually knew, Sam picked up her pad and pen and began scrawling a list. "Groceries—no lima beans," he murmured absently. "You're almost out of everything. . . ."

"Sam," she said, scanning the growing list, "remember, we share costs, although I'll take the bigger share because of the children—"

"You're not paying my way, lady. I take more food than the three of you." Sam pinned her with a deadly gray stare. "Nobody pays my way but me. Got it?"

That evening, Lisa baby-sat while Sam, Dallas and Bertha trekked off to a supermarket, leaving the pickup's oil spots on Dallas's driveway. Sam entered the market with the air of a hunter on safari, checking nutritional values, cost comparing prices with his calculator and eyeing the butcher's thumb suspiciously. "Yuk," he muttered when Dallas deliberately chose a package of lima beans, dropping them into the cart.

"Supermarket Sam Loring" was an encounter that Dallas did not want to repeat. After three laborious hours, she finally pried him away from a maze of household gadgets that intrigued him like a child in a toy department. Looking disgruntled, he whipped out his wallet when the checker totalled the figure.

"Halves," Dallas reminded him, writing a check for her amount.

Sam flipped open his wallet, then paused. Dallas had trimmed his carrying cash and his credit cards were safely tucked away. "We'll calculate later, honey," he said through his teeth, selecting the entire amount needed. "Cute, isn't she?" he asked the checker.

Drained by pulling him away from "really good buys," Dallas wasn't in the mood for chauvinism and wrote her check anyway. She hoped Bertha could be coaxed into returning to her favorite oil spot on the driveway.

The next day, Sam rubbed the back of his neck. At nine o'clock in the morning, he was looking forward to the afternoon when Dallas would begin dissecting his employee-relationship policy.

Sam tapped his pen on his desk. He'd had no idea his employees were unhappy. The thought nagged. He'd always expected more out of himself than others and wasn't aware of any dissatisfaction.

Dallas was good at bringing out dissatisfaction, he noted. A regular virus that ensnared and tormented. If he got any more worked up about cotton flannel nightgowns and rosebuds, he'd break out in a rash.

He was also slightly exhausted, he admitted, glancing ruefully at the paperwork already stacked on his desk. He hadn't had time to work out a schedule for himself, nor a budget. The groceries had swept away a large portion of his weekly allowance, and baby-sitting fees were due Friday. When his host had insisted on repaying him when the wager was finished, Sam's pride had been riffled. He wanted to take care of her, enter her tight little world and fix her thumping dishwasher.

The thought was novel, and Sam turned it over with as much distrust as he would salmon aspic on a bed of watercress. Saturday night, Beau had barely escaped a fist in his lovelorn-puppy face. Clearly, the little wimp had intended to put his lips on Dallas's strawberry ones. Sam scowled at his scarred knuckles, thinking about sinking one short jab in Beau's soft midsection. Dallas's mouth was destined to be his, and so were her other parts. He'd never liked poachers.

Sam had never wanted to place the stamp of his possession on another woman, not even his ex-wife. But Dallas was another matter, and the thought was disquieting. Maybe it was the Christmas season and the enfolding warmth of her home. Or the lack of morning coffee nagging at him. But Dallas's sweet-pea fragrance didn't help, nor did the way she'd looked at him in the bathroom. When he lay before the Seahawk's Sunday game, Sam sensed that Dallas momentarily wanted to slide into his arms. She would, eventually, and the conflicting emotions racing beneath her freckles gave him a shot of pure encouragement.

He wanted to treat her carefully, he decided, rummaging further into his disturbing emotions. It was obvious Dallas had carved out a business and a life-style that worked for her, and he respected that. Flitting happily through her safe, structured life, Dallas had all the markings of the wary.

Sidestepping a variety of entangling situations, Sam recognized those markings. The women in his background were quite happy to go sailing through his bankroll, but Dallas had been clearly offended when he'd offered to pay for the groceries. Dallas had calculated his share of the utility bills, and he had noticed her happy little smirk as he jotted the figure down on a small pad.

Drawing that pad from his pocket, he noted his weekly sum and quietly swallowed. The amount wouldn't cover drinks with a shareholder. Then there was Bertha. Sam flipped to a clean page and scribbled "Oil."

Replacing the pad in his pocket, he patted it. This morning, dressing and delivering the children went smoothly. Winning the wager was a piece of cake.

Sam flipped through the stack of Christmas cards from business associates. Addressed and sent by secretaries, they represented a courtesy rather than a genuine warmth shared on the holiday. In contrast, Dallas's home was warm, filled with scents and children anticipating Santa Claus.

He smiled softly, running his thumb over an embossed Rudolf the Reindeer. He'd have Emily pick up something—

Entering his office, Emily looked down her nose at him and smirked. "As I understand your intentions for the next month, I am not to make nor serve your coffee. Shall we include you in the coffee pool?''

"I'll provide my own. Did you have any other questions about Ms. Pendragon or the situation?''

Emily smiled, for once showing her teeth. Out of necessity, Sam had spread the bare bones of the situation before his secretary and had watched her openly gloat. Her memo to the remainder of the Brice employees included none of the particulars.

"I've informed everyone that they are to cooperate to the fullest with Ms. Pendragon." Her tone inferred that Pendragon would succeed, clearly spelling out his secretary's position in the matter. Sam had the uncomfortable feeling that Emily had coached each employee on the best way to present themselves for the Pendragon research. Franzini was never above stacking the cards to suit herself.

This morning he'd been careful to greet his staff in a method outlined in the Pendragon method. Surely a nod and a curt "Good morning," would earn him a few points on Pendragon's poll.

Beneath her raw-boned appearance, Emily seemed as pleased as a cat with a bowl of cream. "Just a hint, Mr. Loring. Find any coffee station and look for a donation cup. You'll get by for today. Any calls concerning the Pendragon family—Billy and Nikki Pendragon—are to be put immediately through to you," she continued, her teeth glistening.

When he nodded, Emily sniffed, "Children, a home and responsibilities of all the previously mentioned...this should be interesting. By the way, parking-lot maintenance called. Your...truck is gushing oil."

By noon, Sam was tired, splattered with oil from repairing Bertha, and he was starved. He'd spent more than his allotment for lunch on oil. In another hour, Pendragon would appear on his doorstep, digging away at his policies. And he hadn't even planned supper yet.

Thinking of Pendragon somehow eased his empty stomach as he slashed through letters prepared for his signature.

This morning, he'd completely erased Dallas's rude manners and defamatory comments about Bertha. Freshly showered and shaving over the bathroom sink, Sam had left the door open. He'd wanted to catch the children before they woke Dallas. She'd looked strained the night before and he thought she could use the extra fifteen minutes rest.

Barely awake and dressed in her prim gown, Dallas had wandered into the bathroom. She yawned, groaned and began to fill the tub. Sam watched amused as she ran her fingers through her hair and bent to touch her toes. Pausing in midbend, Dallas had straightened slowly, as though afraid what she might see when she awoke fully.

In the steamy mirror, Dallas's gaze widened as it strolled down his bare back to his loose sweat pants, then back up to his lather-covered cheeks. She blinked as though trying to dislodge him from her small, feminine bathroom. As if he were a genie she could blink back into a bottle.

For an instant, Sam had the feeling of soft, shy fingers daintily exploring his backside. Because he wanted the feeling to last, he placed the razor next to her bath powder and turned to face her. Dallas blinked again, stared at his chest intently, then ran her tongue across her soft, parted lips.

Without thinking, Sam reached out, captured her hand and placed it on the damp hairs that seemed to entice her. "You can touch," he offered gallantly before bending to brush her parted lips with his.

Tousled and swathed by yards of violet-kissed flannel, Dallas seemed incredibly sweet and feminine. Sam noted with distraction that he wanted to take care of her, shelter her from her heavy burdens. His momentary notions were old-fashioned, but she did manage to stir him at some level he had long ago buried.

Tasting like strawberries, her lips had barely lifted to his when she stepped back. "Cut it out, Loring," she had snapped between her teeth, her color rising. "I don't come with the wager."

He'd felt a sliver of rage go stabbing through him. For some reason, Dallas deeply resented him.

In the quiet of her office, Dallas paused over rearranging her schedule and idly toyed with the biofeedback hand monitor as she thought of Sam. She had to spend a whole month sidestepping his sizeable body in her house.

The monitor fitted neatly in her palm as she remembered his sexy smile in the bathroom as he invited her palm to his chest. Listening to the monitor's rising whine, Dallas shook her head. Living next door to the Deons was dangerous; their newlywed hormonal imbalance seeping over to her home had taken its toil.

Rawly masculine, Sam wasn't anything like Douglas or Beau; he was more like T.J. She'd learned her lesson well and didn't intend to repeat it.

Except Sam had taken exquisite care to kiss her gently, brushing her lips softly, wooing a response from her.

Wooing, she repeated darkly, and rubbed her aching temple. Loring crashed through homes decorated with Christmastide. He'd obviously lured her mother into a leering, plotting relationship.

Dallas squeezed the monitor, oblivious to its rising protest. When he wanted to, Sam pulled out the enticing Southern male act, complete with dimples and lazy drawl.

Come here, sweet pea, he had murmured in a soft, Southern-night tone that could melt any woman's resistance.

She didn't want to respond to anything concerning him, not even the wistful comment about always wanting a toy train.

Sam was a player; she'd have to remember that when he pulled out the dimples or exposed his broad, hair-covered chest in her bathroom. He'd use the sentimentality of Christmas or any means at hand to disarm her, including a weakness for oversized men who loved chocolate cake.

Who else had discovered Sam's appetites? she wondered in a brief whimsy that she forced down.

The whole problem stemmed from the holiday season and the newlywed sexual seepage from the Deons. For some reason, when she came near Sam, she started breathing deeply. She'd badly wanted to rummage through those damp, intriguing whorls matting his chest. She'd wanted to place her lips against his skin. If he hadn't leaned toward her, startling her at that confusing moment, she might have obeyed her impulses.

Her head ached, probably from too many impulses. In her hand, the monitor throbbed loudly and Dallas tossed it to her desk. Sam had a lot to learn about playing with her, because she intended to win. If he thought he could manipulate her with sex, he was wrong—she'd already had that unexciting, frustrating education. Shuffling through the poll sheets prepared for Brice workers, Dallas smiled grimly...it was her game all the way. While Sam was studying Laundry 101 and Pot Roast Lab and dealing with baby-sitters, sniffles and bears, she would tear his theories about the uselessness of stress-management policies to itsy-bitsy shreds.

That afternoon, as she interviewed Brice employees, Dallas ignored the glowering look Sam cast in her direction when he passed frequently. Rather like an eagle waiting for an adventuresome mouse to cross his territory. She smiled sweetly, nodding and acknowledging his presence before turning back to her task.

As she interviewed Virginia, a secretary with three children and no husband, Dallas sensed a bristling presence behind her. When she turned, Sam loomed over her. His collar was open, his usually neat tie awry. Three new shaving nicks occupied his taut jaw, and his scowl was genuinely, magnificently unhappy. Spattered with oil, his shirt sleeves rolled back, he looked thunderous. "Everything going okay?" he asked gruffly, in true bear manner.

His eyes slashed at her neat white blouse and paisley puff tie, cutting away at the sensible gray business jacket and skirt to her black pumps.

"We're getting along nicely. Peachy," she added, relishing his hell-of-a-day look. He wouldn't last the month—two weeks at the most. The employees were excited, and the Brice experiment was in the palm of her hand.

This morning when he'd carried the sleepy, protesting children out to the car, Sam had been given a grace period: Billy didn't need another bathroom visit and Nikki had remembered her favorite doll.

Sam glanced at the office wall clock, then ran his big hand through his already mussed hair. "I have a conference at two," he muttered absently, glancing down at the oil stains on his slacks. "I'll have someone bring these pants to the cleaners or send someone home to get my others— What are you grinning at, Pendragon?"

"Ah-ah," she said lightly. "You handle your own personal items, remember?"

Sam shot her a look of pure deadly frustration. "This is business, Dallas. A matter of big bucks. Understand?"

Enjoying watching him squirm, Dallas braced her hip against Virginia's desk and folded her arms. "Tough," she said after a long, tense moment when the worker stared, fascinated with the exchange shooting over her desk like hot lead.

"In my office." Sam spaced the words out in deadly precison as his neck seemed to lower into his broad shoulders.

"When I'm finished. Virginia and I are calculating if she'd have enough time to work out and shower during lunch hour," Dallas returned evenly, watching him. Sam in a snit was quite capable of making a scene and she wanted to delve into the problem of the employees with little disturbance. Knowing their boss was unhappy, the staff might not respond openly.

But the matter of Sam's growling and menacing her was another matter. One that chafed. Thumping her fingers lightly against her arms, Dallas allowed herself a tiny, grim smile. Sam might push his employees around, but he couldn't get used to the idea that she was her own—

"Umph!" Dallas gasped as Sam grabbed her hand and yanked her into his office. He kicked the door shut, locked it, picked her up and plopped her bottom down on his desk.

Dallas's hand went flashing through the air before she considered the consequences. The blow to his face caused her palm to burn. "How dare you?"

"You really get to me, Pendragon. This time you just asked for it," he muttered tightly before reaching for her.

Dallas caught a quick image of thick, black eyebrows and stormy gray eyes as his arms went around her, lifting her up. Sam's mouth settled heavily upon hers, his hand cradling the back of her head as he positioned her for a long, deep kiss. Surrounded by the warmth and strength of him, she barely felt her shoes drop to the floor.

She tried to protest.

She tried to ignore how much her body loved the encroaching warmth of his, how it fitted neatly into the hard planes.

His fingers moved on her scalp, soothing her as his breath stroked her cheek unevenly; his other hand slid to cup her buttocks, lifting her to him.

Sam's mouth moved over hers hungrily... as though he needed her desperately. Dallas felt herself moving into his demand, needing to ease the loneliness she felt within him. Sam ached with a cold void, carried it within him, and hid it successfully from the world.

But she knew now how much he needed her warmth. Dallas absorbed his pain, taking it into her and soothing it. Sam needed gentle care and she knew instinctively how to provide it.

Dallas eased her fingers through his hair, framing his face. Gently she lifted and fitted her parted lips to his.

Sam's kiss was pure possession, a man staking his rights on his woman.

Something went happily skipping through Dallas when? he groaned deep in his throat, a hungry sound as he urged her body to come closer.

That was the last sweet sensible thought she remembered as his tongue gently probed her lips, asking entry. Sam, for all his threatening savagery, was asking for her response. He was exposing his soul to her and asking for little in return.

Dallas locked her arms around his neck and proceeded to care for Sam. She gave him little, nibbling kisses. She caressed the back of his taut neck and smoothed the crisp dark hair growing there.

Intent upon her task, she didn't notice the stillness in him nor the gentle answering pressure of his mouth responding to hers. She barely noticed his arms gathering her closer as he leaned back against the desk, fitting her between his thighs.

Sam rubbed her cheek with his, easing toward her throat, and Dallas sighed, surrounded by the heat seeping into her. His mouth caressed her skin, and she gave him access by snuggling to his wide shoulder. Sam just seemed so safe.

His teeth tugged on her earlobe and a stirring warmth went soaring through her. She moved closer to the heat, parting her lips as his tongue again gently probed them.

When her tongue shyly met his, Sam slanted his lips against hers, his tongue entering her mouth. The moist, gentle flicking tasted her, teased her, and Dallas responded to the sweetness of the temptation. His hands moved over her, light, caressing and smoothing down the front of her blouse. She was too warm, she realized distantly, relieved when he removed her suit jacket.

Somehow her fingers had nudged aside Sam's tie, unbuttoned and removed his shirt, then slid to his chest. It seemed only fair that the large hands shaping her waist and tugging at her blouse should explore her.

He breathed unevenly as his calloused palms moved leisurely, comfortingly against her back, stroking the long line gently, firmly. Dallas had the image of being petted and cherished and enjoyed. Of being tasted. She sank deeper into the feeling, trembling a little as Sam's hands eased upward to cover her breasts.

His fingers smoothed the sensible cotton, easing it gently aside as his kiss deepened and lured her on. With a desperate need to accept his offer, Dallas drew him closer, fitting her mouth to the sweet enticement.

Sam did have an enticing body, she realized as she stroked the hair-covered, hard surface of his chest. As she snuggled more closely against his hands, his fingers found the tips of her taut breasts and tantalized them lightly. Dallas sighed, allowing him to slide her free from her confining blouse and bra.

Lifting and turning her slightly, Sam nibbled a trail downward, warming her shoulders, her chest. Dallas loved the soothing, the gentle warming of her skin as she stroked his bare back. He rippled when she touched him, she discovered, following the hard muscles flowing beneath his hot skin.

When Sam's mouth gently found her softness, exploring it, Dallas gasped. The exquisite feeling he caused when he gently suckled the hardened tip loosed a savage, hungry heat.

"Oh, Sam," she found herself sighing against his hair, giving herself more fully to him. Her wandering hands had found his taut stomach, and the tense muscles quivered beneath her light stroking.

"Sweet pea," he rasped deeply against her hot skin, kissing his way back up to her mouth. Placing her arms around him, Sam eased his warm chest against her sensitized breasts, then slowly lowered his lips to hers.

He sighed lightly, as though the softness resting against his brought him sheer pleasure.

The sound brought her hunger leaping to the surface. Her nails drew lines down his back, urging him closer as Sam's hands swept lower to smooth her hips and thighs.

Sliding upward beneath her skirt, Sam's hands were warm and secure, gentle and caressing. Taking his time, he flipped open the snap to her hose. Pressing warmly against her inner thighs, Sam's fingertips trembled. They moved too slowly for the hunger careening through her as he removed her garter belt.

Slipping a finger under the elastic of her cotton briefs, Sam traced the sensitive area.

"Ohh," she sighed helplessly as he softly tantalized her warmth. Then she was desperate for his touch to fill the void within her. Sliding her breasts against his chest until he sighed that deep, raspy hungry sigh that so surprised her, Dallas found herself moving against the delicate brush of his fingers.

Her lungs ached with the air she had been holding as those enticing fingers moved, exploring her. She bit his shoulder then, desperate for the tantalizing intimacy, and he inhaled sharply as her teeth nibbled a trail across the taut line. Dallas's tongue flicked the warm, slightly salted surface, and she realized distantly that she loved his taste.

Barely aware of being lowered to the lush carpeting behind Sam's desk, Dallas curled to his warmth, nuzzling the pelt covering his chest. She tasted the flat male nipple, delighted with his response. She gently nipped at the nub, scouting it intently.

When he groaned, a raw sigh of pleasure and delight, Dallas smiled against his chest. Sam's arms around her were rigid, his fingers trembling. Fitting herself over him, Dallas had a distant memory of being forcefully pinned beneath a sweaty male body. And the taunts, reminding her of a woman's place. The memory flitted quietly away as Sam's fingers found her intimately. Again her teeth nipped his hard shoulder as a hot surge of pleasure went ricocheting through her.

"Dallas," she heard him groan helplessly before the heat swept over her in waves. She held him closely, an anchor in her first voyage in sensual seas.

Dallas rose to the heat, sought it, drew it into her exquisitely. She sought his mouth, exploring it as a wave of unexpected pleasure crashed over her. Running her palms down his body, she delighted in the hardness of his thighs covered by his slacks, the restless surging of his hips as the second wave caught her broadside, causing her to tense, hoarding the full throbbing head within.

Beneath her, he trembled, breathing unevenly, his face hot against hers as she fell delicately, softly from the crest of a wave. When Sam eased her down beside him, Dallas wondered helplessly if her flesh was feverish over her seemingly limp bones. She needed every ounce of her willpower to lift her hand and stroke his lean, rough cheek. Dazed by her own emotions, Dallas knew that Sam needed her soft touch. She stroked his damp brow, his mussed hair and taut cords standing out in relief on his shoulders.

Sam needed petting. Poor Sam.

His hands were gentle now as he turned her to him. He watched her as though he was turning over his thoughts carefully... examining each one with methodical precision. Tenderly, he eased a damp strand of hair away from her flushed cheek, and drew her palm up to kiss it. Over their hands, his smoky eyes held hers, promising things she couldn't dissect. Private things. Intimate things with dark, heated passages that excited her, leaving her breathless.

After a lingering survey of her face, Sam's gaze swept to her breasts. When she moved to cover herself, he tugged his shirt across her protectively. Sam eased her closer to his taut body, giving her shelter against the cold. The movement reminded her of gallantry and possession.

He rocked her slightly, and Dallas allowed her cheek to rest upon his chest. She liked being folded to him and listened to his heart beating loudly beneath her. Sliding downward, his palm flattened against her spine until her upper thighs pocketed his bold shape.

He thrust against her, watching her reaction.

"Oh, my," she whispered shakily between lips that were sensitive and swollen. "Oh, my," she repeated, realizing the carpeting waited at her back and the hard look Sam continued to rake over her. "Oh, my," she repeated a third time, scrambling out of his arms and clutching his shirt to her as she stood.

"Yes. Oh, my. Surprise isn't the word, is it?" Sam's tone mocked with grin lines as he rose slowly to his feet. When he took one menacing step toward her, Dallas's eyes flowed downward involuntarily and widened.

"If you say, 'Oh, my,' one more time, sweet pea..." Sam murmured as she pivoted from him and the blatant evidence of her maiden flight into passion.

While Seattle sprawled beyond the corporate building swathed in cold winter drizzle, Dallas shook with the knowledge that she had bitten Sam savagely, attacking him on the floor with obvious sexual intent.

She shivered, tugging his shirt closer and catching the scent of his body. The shirt reminded her of how she had— She pressed her lids closed, trying to erase the image of Sam's bare, damp chest and the tiny red marks on his broad shoulders from her teeth and nails. And the sensual, well-kissed fullness of his hard mouth.

"Oh!" she gasped quietly, fighting the realization that she had never allowed herself to— "Oh," she groaned, frustrated. If ever she wanted to taste passion, it wasn't at this time of her life. Just when everything had settled down nicely. And she definitely didn't want to experience anything intimate with Sam.

His body heat warmed her back, seeping into her skin as she had wanted to seep into his. "Those are lots of little *Oh*s," Sam murmured quietly behind her. "Here, get into this," he ordered, easing her into her bra and blouse.

Though she was grateful, Dallas shivered and avoided looking at him. She resented the certainly of his hands, deftly fitting her into her clothing. She resented his experienced lovemaking and her naive response to his skills. She resented trembling so hard she couldn't button her blouse and the easy way his hands performed the task.

She resented the shirt he had drawn on, covering the chest that condemned her from beneath the fine cotton. She looked away from his throat, which bore a shaving nick— and the reddened imprint of her teeth.

Yes, become a Silhouette subscriber and the celebration goes on forever.

To begin with, we'll send you:
4 new Silhouette Desire® novels—FREE

an elegant Victorian picture frame—FREE

an exciting mystery bonus—FREE

And that's not all! Special extras— Three more reasons to celebrate.

4. **FREE Home Delivery!** That's right! We'll send you 4 **FREE** books, and you'll be under no obligation to purchase any in the future. You may keep the books and return the accompanying statement marked cancel.

If we don't hear from you, about a month later we'll send you six additional novels to read and enjoy. If you decide to keep them, you'll pay the low subscribers'-only discount price of just $2.24* each—that's 26¢ less than the cover price—AND there's no extra charge for delivery! There are no hidden extras! **You may cancel at any time!** But as long as you wish to continue, every month we'll send you six more books, which you can purchase or return at our cost, cancelling your subscription.

5. **Free Monthly Newsletter!** It's the indispensable insiders' look at our most popular writers and their upcoming novels. Now you can have a behind-the-scenes look at the fascinating world of Silhouette! It's an added bonus you'll look forward to every month!

6. **More Surprise Gifts!** Because our home subscribers are our most valued readers, we'll be sending you additional free gifts from time to time—as a token of our appreciation.

FREE! VICTORIAN PICTURE FRAME!

This lovely Victorian pewter-finish miniature is perfect for
displaying a treasured photograph—and it's yours absolutely
free—when you accept our no-risk offer.

SILHOUETTE DESIRE®

FREE OFFER CARD

**4 FREE
BOOKS**

**VICTORIAN
PICTURE
FRAME—FREE**

**FREE MYSTERY
BONUS**

PLACE
YOUR
BALLOON
STICKER
HERE!

**FREE
HOME DELIVERY**

**FREE FACT-FILLED
NEWSLETTER**

**MORE
SURPRISE GIFTS
THROUGHOUT
THE YEAR—FREE**

YES! Please send me my four Silhouette Desire® novels FREE, along with my Victorian
picture frame and my free mystery gift, as explained on the opposite page. I understand that
accepting these books and gifts places me under no obligation ever to buy any books. I may
cancel at any time for any reason, and the free books and gifts will be mine to keep!

225 CIS JAZN (U-SIL-D-12/90)

NAME _____

(PLEASE PRINT)

ADDRESS _____ APT _____

CITY _____ STATE _____

ZIP _____

SILHOUETTE "NO RISK GUARANTEE"
• There's no obligation to buy — the free books and gifts
remain yours to keep.
• You receive books before they're available in stores.
• You may end your subscription
anytime — just by letting us know.

PRINTED IN U.S.A.

FILL OUT THIS POSTPAID CARD AND MAIL TODAY!

BUSINESS REPLY MAIL
FIRST CLASS MAIL   PERMIT NO. 717   BUFFALO, NY

POSTAGE WILL BE PAID BY ADDRESSEE

SILHOUETTE READER SERVICE
3010 WALDEN AVE
PO BOX 1867
BUFFALO NY 14240-9952

NO POSTAGE
NECESSARY
IF MAILED
IN THE
UNITED STATES

"Well," she began airily, hoping he wouldn't notice the husky, emotional tone underlying her bravado. "That was...pleasant. But now that we've dispensed with that—"

"It isn't the end of the world," he said quietly as he finished buttoning her blouse. Avoiding his eyes, Dallas allowed herself a glimpse of those large, dark hands as they completed the task.

The backs were scarred and lightly covered with dark hair. They weren't a lover's gentle hands, yet Sam had touched her lightly, reverently, allowing her to set the pace. His fingers trembled slightly, and she savored the knowledge that he was affected. By her. Because of her.

He hadn't touched her as though she were a body to be used.

Sam had touched her as though she were made of sheer silk and spiderweb lace and he was frightened of hurting her. "We'll both live, Dallas. Don't make too much of it," he whispered gently as his fingers misplaced a button. Clumsily, he corrected the error.

His gentleness caused the tear that had been waiting beneath her eyelids to come oozing out, spilling down her cheek. Horrified, she watched it dampen the hair on his shaking hand, and then Sam took her slowly, safely into his arms. "Come on, sweet pea," he whispered raggedly against her cheek, rocking her almost awkwardly, as though he seldom offered comfort. Or had been offered comfort.

"I'll get you for this," she promised shakily, unable to move away from his warmth. She doubted her legs would support her in one retreating step.

Sam's hand stopped stroking the taut line of her back. "Me? I think you've misplaced the guilt. You're like some damned fever virus—"

Taking a deep, steadying breath, Dallas stepped away from him, not shielding the frustration rocking her. She'd been safe, tucked away in her structured world, and then Sam came plunging merrily through the protective layers. "You'll pay for this," she threatened again.

"You think I'm not?" he asked wryly, glancing downward.

She refused to follow his gaze, focusing instead on his dark, rigid features. Her hand shook traitorously, wanting to trace the bold lines of his face. "Don't try anything like this again," she stated from between her teeth. "I've got you pegged."

Those smoky gray eyes lit and slashed at her. "If you think I planned—"

"Didn't you?" she asked quietly, thrusting a shaking hand through her hair as T.J.'s remarks came slithering back to haunt her. "Oh, didn't you? Isn't it a fact that chauvinists prefer women on their backs—"

He frowned, leaning toward her. "Let's check that position again, Pendragon. You were *on me*," he clarified. "Don't say another word, Dallas. If you're smart, you'll straighten up in the washroom and walk out of here. Now. Otherwise—" He glanced meaningfully at the desktop.

When Dallas's eyes widened, he thrust her jacket and tie into her hands as though they were criminal evidence marked "Exhibit A."

Glancing at Sam's dark scowl, Dallas took the wiser option and walked toward the washroom with as much dignity as she could muster. With her hand on the safety of the doorknob, she turned slightly. "Sneaky," she said, and meant it.

"The hell I am!" he snapped belligerently.

"Are too."

"Am not!" he snapped loudly as the lock clicked behind her.

Six

An hour later, Sam cheated on the wager and didn't care. Punching the bag in his private gym, he jabbed and sweated. Then he continued, the physical exhaustion trimming the raw edge off his desire for Dallas Pendragon. "Pendragon *is* a virus. She's getting to me," he said through gritted teeth as he dug deeper into his reserves, fighting her and himself as he pounded away at the bag.

Okay, he'd been around long enough to know better.

Dallas Pendragon wasn't aware of her latent sensuality. She didn't know what soft hands and softer surprised cries did to a man who'd kept his emotions in tight rein.

She needed protecting from men who might take advantage of her.

Damn. He intended to be one of those men.

Men? As in plural? He battered the bag, dancing around it.

"So why am I worrying about her? She's an adult with the right equipment...." Sam threw a series of hard one-two punches at the bag, feeling angry, frustrated and sexually

deprived. He ached from his scalp downward and wondered if his basic body inventory would ever be the same.
The first chance he got after this mess, he was taking a solid
week off to accept Delilah Philburn's invitation into her
bed. He felt he'd been set up by his body, betrayed by sexual abstinence. Evidently he wasn't as over-the-hill as he
thought.

He'd avoided sweet little innocent things with a stubborn
dedication, knowing that they were really lace-trimmed
landmines of destruction.

He began cursing viciously, timing the phrases to the hard
punches. He'd tasted her silky soft skin, had been caught in
the scents of sweet peas and Appalachia mountain air. When
she'd sighed, the sound filled him with a taste of all he ever
wanted.

Sam jabbed at the bag, classifying himself as, "Damned
lump of two-hundred-pound putty."

He could still feel her body ripple, contracting and heat-
ing against him. Sam wanted to fill her with himself, let her
make him a part of her world. Let that heat make him warm
for the first time in his entire life. She'd been stunned by the
passion, and he had wanted to comfort her. To fold her in
his arms and tell her it was all right.

Well, it wasn't. None of it.

Angry with her and frustrated by the hectic morning, Sam
hadn't meant for the scene behind his desk to occur. Dallas
just seemed to—respond, damn it!

Ignite was a better word.

Breathing hard, Sam stepped back from the bag. Dallas
could reach right inside him and tear him apart if he
weren't careful. There was something inside him long forgotten and it was too vulnerable to be exposed to her dangerous virus. Why was she getting to him anyway?

Lowering his head, Sam punched the bag as though it
were his worst demon.

Beneath her obvious business savvy, Dallas was sweet.
Feeling guilty for glimpsing something she didn't know
herself, feeling guilty for having caused it, Sam knew he'd

have to watch himself. Because there would be hell to pay when Dallas knew exactly how potent she was.

His fist slammed into the bag as though it were Beau's face. Once the business community discovered the experiment, as Sam knew they would a là Franzini, he'd have his hands full of protecting her. Or them.

How the hell was he supposed to know that the clerical staff was under stress?

At five-thirty that afternoon, Dallas spread her hands over the Brice polls covering her office desk. Without a doubt, they demonstrated the necessity of job-sharing, a child-care center, a business day—a paid day off so that employees could conduct personal business—a fitness program and lastly, a sabbatical after five years on the job. She clicked on her computer and started working on outlines for each project.

Her mother had promised to check on Sam's progress tonight. That left the evening free for her to scrape away at Sam's corporate management-employee plans. She had three weeks to prove her theories were right—that stress-relieved employees meant less absenteeism and more productivity, keeping the turnover to a minimum.

Fifteen percent of Brice's clerical staff would qualify for her job-sharing program. They had volunteered to act in a pilot program, which Dallas worked out easily. It was simply a matter of scheduling and fitting workers together into a single, effective niche. The business day off was also a matter of scheduling; but the child-care center and physical-fitness programs demanded cost estimates. She needed architectural guidance for the proper remodeling; the child-care center would require proper staffing and furniture.

She tapped a worker's comment with her finger. "Mr. Loring wants a well-oiled organization and honestly, the pay is good. It's just that we're not all twenty-four-hour workaholics like him. We have families and other commitments, while Brice is his whole life."

How sad, Dallas mused for a moment. As a temporarily adopted father, Sam fitted into Nikki and Billy's lives perfectly.

As a pseudo house husband, Sam showed definite, endearing moments of confusion mixed with a determination to succeed.

As a man, he was too experienced. Sam Loring was the original type who preferred classy, worldly blondes.

Then why had he kissed her? She traced the shape of her mouth, thinking of his firm one. He had tasted just right.

She couldn't afford to get mixed up with his preferences.

Sam's kisses had big, fat motives written all over them. But now that she knew exactly how underhanded he could be when losing, she'd watch him closer.

If he just didn't have that scruffy I've-never-been-hugged look.

Dallas winced at that thought and began typing. According to Seattle business gossip, Sam's business practices made rawhide look soft. "It must be the season," she muttered. "After this is over, I'm treating myself to a whole box of chocolate-covered cherries."

Added to the challenge of integrating the Brice master plan, she tucked in a neat little stress education package for management. Tentatively titled The Whammy Plan, it needed more work and would be more difficult.

She began entering another poll into the computer, one that dealt with scheduled work loads and management courtesy to employees.

At eight-thirty, she rubbed the nape of her neck, leaned back in her chair and tried not to think about Sam.

While she tried not to think of the way his mouth warmed hers, cherishing, she fought the restlessness in her body. Dallas picked up a note, crushed it and tossed it into the trash. The most shameless thing about the entire scene was the way she could have actually ripped off his clothes.

He'd planned the whole disgusting thing, of course. Sam wouldn't wait for her to fail at the project—he'd be pushing, trying to get her back against the wall.

When the phone rang at ten o'clock, Dallas had just turned off her computer. She answered it absently, her eyes feeling gritty and her body heavy with fatigue.

"Dallas?" Sam's deep tone slid over the lines. "Are you all right?"

Nettled that he had invaded her domain, Dallas snapped, "Why wouldn't I be?"

On the other end of the line, he breathed once, deeply as though trying to control himself. "Get home," he ordered curtly before disconnecting the line.

"Look you oversized . . . I'm not on a curfew—"

Then Dallas stilled, mentally rapping off the things that could make Sam call her. When she'd called earlier, Nikki and Billy were excited, shrieking with delight as Sam fought the bubbles flowing out of the washer. They'd be asleep now—unless Sam didn't fare well on his bear hunt.

Tearing out of her office, Dallas crossed Seattle traffic in record time and came to a screeching, skidding stop just inches from Bertha's rusty back bumper. She ignored the Deons making out beneath their doorway mistletoe ball and concentrated on the waiting disaster . . . children's cuts, fevers, accidents. . . .

The Christmas lights sparkled on her tree and the house was just as welcoming as ever—except Sam lurked in the open doorway. Baghdad seemed to grin, hanging from Sam's large hand and twitching his tail.

Hurrying up the steps, Dallas listened for crying and looked for the distraught children. "What's wrong?" she asked, rushing past Sam's imposing bulk into the house.

Peeling off her coat and kicking off her heels, Dallas rushed into the children's room to find them sleeping peacefully, undisturbed by bears. She padded over to them, looked for dried tear trails and found none. Kissing each warm cheek, Dallas eased out of the room.

Standing in the center of her living room, hands on hips, Sam glowered at her. In socks, jeans and a T-shirt, his hair mussed and a beard threatening his hard jaw, Sam was both fierce and—

Ignoring the patch of faded red on his cotton shirt, Dallas didn't want to think about the "and" part. She'd experienced enough of the "and" part on the floor behind his desk. "Why did you call me?"

Sam glared at her for a full minute, then stalked into the kitchen, leaving her to follow. A burned odor clung to the potpourri scents in his wake. His open briefcase sat on the table, papers scattered around it and a collection of recipe books stacked to one side. She noted the tabs marking the cookbooks and his glasses tossed carelessly aside. Working at the kitchen counter, Sam's large body was tense beneath the cotton T-shirt. His muscles rippled as he filled a plate and placed it in the microwave oven. She looked away from the marks her teeth had caused on his neck.

"Dinner is cold," he muttered ominously, setting the timer. "I expected you home before six."

The odd tone of frustration and anger surprised Dallas. She'd heard it before—from Lisa. She tossed that disquieting thought aside. Sam was just interested in making her play jumping frog. "I had work to do. Is anything wrong with Nikki or Billy?" she asked again, suspecting Sam's motives.

"Not a damn thing," he muttered in the tone of a person whose nose was definitely out of joint. "I spent the better part of an hour on supper. The kids appreciated my hamburger specialty anyway."

Sam's stare accused her of an unspecified crime. "You'd better not have eaten," he stated in that junkyard dog growl of his.

"You called me away from work for that?" Dallas glanced at the set of his shoulders and took a deep breath. She'd just left a string of potential accidents in her wake across Seattle for an executive who had cooked a hamburger. She'd been dangled at the end of one man's string and she hadn't forgotten the feeling. "We'll talk about this after I change," she said more quietly than she felt.

"You have one minute."

Sam began setting a place for her, and the odd sight of a man in her kitchen, preparing her supper rather than demanding it, surprised her. She closed her parted lips and walked into the safety of her bedroom to change into her yellow sweatsuit.

At the table, she picked at the immense hamburger and scalloped potatoes. While she debated entering a discussion about emergencies, Sam carefully placed her cup of tea at her side. "Here. You've had a hard day," he said as though resenting it and her.

Drinking beer from a bottle, Sam sprawled on the chair opposite her. "Where were you all night?" he asked quietly, toying with the fringes of her place mat.

"At the office. Working on proposals. What did you burn?" While Dallas realized Sam had fought bears, washing machines and prepared supper, he didn't own her time.

"About a pound of hamburger." His fingers moved restlessly across the mat. "So how is the usurping coming? Anything you need to discuss?"

Dallas dismissed the thought that Sam needed her attention. It would be his style to try to get a jump on her plans and waylay them. "I'm not ready for a presentation yet. The dinner is lovely. Thank you," she added, relying on manners when she really wanted to start something dark and ugly.

"You're welcome," he returned formally, sliding a finger across the back of her hand. "You look tired. Are you all right?"

The question was spoken in his deepest Southern drawl, throwing her back into the afternoon.

She'd been out of control, needing him—giving him too much of herself. She'd done that once and ended up with enough scars to last a lifetime.

She jerked back from his touch, cleaning off the table with a flourish to disguise the way he'd upset her. As she scraped the dishes, Dallas knew she was overreacting. "Fine. I have work to do, you know. Classes and your project."

Behind her, Sam leaned close as he whispered ominously, "Any night you're supposed to be in your office, you'd better damn well be. Call me when you leave, and if you stop along the way, let me know." The tone sounded like the Mounties, the Cavalry, and the Green Berets would all be out turning over Seattle pavements for her.

Dallas was no longer tired and worried. She whipped around to face him. "If you have a problem with my lifestyle, you're going to have to swallow it."

Placing his hands on the counter on either side of her hips, Sam lowered his head toward her. "Lisa and the kids were worried."

She noted the lines around his eyes and the uncompromising set of his mouth. A muscle, covered by dark skin and rough stubble, contracted in a jaw that looked like granite. She didn't feel exactly sweet herself. "Lay off, Loring. I've managed without you for years, you know. My mother and the children both know this happens occasionally—"

"I'm not your mother. Nor your children," he said too quietly. "You call me."

"Sam, if you're asking for trouble, I'm just in the mood to give it to you," she returned just as quietly, lifting her chin. "Back off."

"I'll bet you don't have to tell that to Beau," he said in a nasty tone, glaring down at her.

"Don't you have things to do?" she asked sweetly, wondering if she could wrap her hands around his thick, muscular neck and squeeze slowly. "Washing? Scrubbing the bathroom floor? Picking up trucks and dolls?"

"I've done all that," he said in a different soft tone, looking at her mouth. "What do you want for supper tomorrow night?"

"Anything," she responded, thinking of his mouth on hers earlier. He had such a nice mouth, firm, and delightfully tasty when he— She nudged his chest sharply with her shoulder and surprisingly, he stepped away. The knowledge that Sam could be so easily dislodged was somehow disquieting. "I'm having another cup of tea in my room. Privately."

"Fine. You do that." She didn't trust his easy tone as she walked away from him into the sanctity of her bedroom.

Lisa called at eleven-fifteen. Lying amidst her favorite magazines, twisted in her rosebud sheets, Dallas turned off her lamp and lit her favorite scented candle while she talked with her mother. Lisa's calls were uncanny, perfectly timed for sleepless nights. Sam roamed around the house apparently doing house things; the basement stairs creaking beneath his weight.

"Sam is such a sweetheart...has he gone to bed?" Lisa crooned over the line as Dallas watched the flickering candle flame. The scent and the aura spreading over her delicate room was soothing in contrast to the whole, tense day. Especially after she learned that Sam knew how to warm carpeting.

Concentrating on the flame, Dallas tried to ignore the sound of things being moved in her basement. Big things with motors that started reluctantly. "He's playing with Daddy's tools."

"Of course, dear. I thought he'd seek them out. Real men always do. They're really just toys to men. Nothing makes them happier than puttering around...." Lisa hesitated, then added, "Well, maybe a romp in bed. Those tools...I just couldn't part with them, and knowing that you're keeping them makes me feel better. How's your work at Brice going?"

A saw buzzed directly beneath Dallas, then stopped. She took a deep breath. "I'll be working nights at the office, weekends, too. With Lettie and Sybil filling in for me at the daytime stress classes, I've got a neat margin of time—" Another, smaller saw began ripping through the silence, then ended quickly. "Mother, can I call you tomorrow?"

Dallas listened to another motor chug gently beneath her bed and groaned, tugging her pillow over her head.

* * *

Friday morning, Sam faced the board in Brice's spacious conference room. "I admit going out on a ledge without presenting the package to the board. Dallas Pendragon is doing nothing more than exploring our management techniques for stress problems. She won't find any . . . and when her project is completed, Brice will still stand. Things of this nature are generally too time consuming to discuss before quarterly reports."

He recognized the men's closed-door expressions. Sam nodded briefly to Edward Swearingen, a man he deeply respected, though they had business differences. At sixty-five, Edward was a burly, six-footer who moved like a dancer. One of his base life theories was that every man needed a good woman. Sam immediately had pegged Edward as being in favor of the stress-management program.

Jerry Keys leaned in his chair and folded his hands across his rounded stomach. "Pendragon is asking a lot of questions, has an architect rummaging around the place and has generally shot the way of things to hell. She's driving personnel nuts, asking about methods of testing, employee backgrounds and the like. What the hell do her 'family profiles' have to do with a workplace?"

Shifting uneasily, Sam frowned at the scars on his knuckles. He'd seen some of the worker's interviews and was stunned with the results. He drove himself harder than anyone on staff, not asking them to do anything he hadn't done himself. Big, ugly terms like "burnout," "feeling stretched" and "pressure at work is affecting personal relationships," stood out like tombstones.

The whole interviewing matter had Dallas uncapping a volcano of complaints. Sam ground his teeth together and felt the muscles in his neck tense as they did when he was about to take a hard punch to the jaw. He'd had no idea about the amount of worker discontent.

Francis Tome leaned forward, tapping his pencil. "She's real trouble, Sam. Has a nose for seeking out what might appeal to the general staff. She's got to be shut down be-

fore she does any real damage. I've heard about this stress
bunk before. This fiscal period we can't afford to go rummaging around financing employee stress-free environ-
ments.''

The thought that he'd been mentioned in the polls as a
major cause of worker's stress caused Sam's stomach to
contract. Was a "piece of concrete machinery driven by
productivity charts" really how they saw him?

Looking up from his papers, Edward Swearingen noted,
"Pendragon has got some good ideas. I've known her
mother for years and understand that Dallas is an enter-
prising young woman. Her beliefs just might be valid and
need attention.''

Leaning back in his chair at the head of Brice's sprawling
walnut table, Sam thought about Mullens, the male architect Dallas had hired to do estimates, and wanted to start
punching something with bones and flesh and a California
grin. Mullens was a lady's man, an aging surfer with too-
tight jeans who managed to be the center of the secretaries'
huddle. Dallas didn't seem to mind Mullens hovering over
her, nor the way his head bent near hers.

Once, Sam had caught Dallas smothering a giggle as
Mullens whispered in her ear. He had just started toward
them when Dallas smiled brightly at him, "Problems,
Sam?''

Of course, he had problems. A man didn't wait for a
woman every night, launder her practical cotton underwear and share her kids' sniffles without having Big Problems.

The honeymooners next door were driving him nuts, and
he wanted to chew steel.

He needed to call Delilah and hire a babysitter. When a
virus invaded a man's system, he took steps to waylay it.

Maybe he just needed to hear the little noises Dallas made
at the back of her throat when he tasted her skin. God, they
were sweet sounds—aching and encouraging.

"... We all know you're living with Pendragon, Sam. But business is business," Ben Thompsen stated, slamming his open hand on the table.

"What's that?" Sam asked, leaving the image of Dallas's pale flesh and returning to the board room. He felt slightly guilty, as though he'd exposed his woman to voyeurs. To cover his uneasiness, Sam sighted down on Thompsen.

The younger man shifted slightly, tugging at his tie.

"What's the story?" another board member asked. "I've never known your private life to interfere with business before Sam."

Emily suddenly began refilling the water glasses and coffee cups. And Sam felt as though the Indians were circling his wagon train, closing in for the kill. Or was it vultures over near-dead prey? Loosening his tie and flicking open the top buttons of his shirt, Sam glanced uneasily at her. Emily had a way of baring her fangs without changing her expression.

He explained the wager quickly, ignoring the speculative light behind Emily's glasses.

Ike Ramsey leered, nodding. "Hell of a setup, man."

"That's a new one," another man added, chuckling.

"Sweet," a third voice commented. "No wonder you've been looking like hell lately. Worn out as hell."

Emily accidentally spilled hot coffee on the man's hand and he yelped. "Sorry," she murmured without remorse, sweeping on down the table.

When Sam stood, slowly stripping off his jacket and rolling up his sleeves, the board members sat up straighter, their grins dying. Turning his back to them, Sam heard a sudden hushed round of exclamations as he looked out over the drizzle and the fog shrouding Brice's top floor.

Turning slowly back to the men, Sam leveled a hard stare at each member. "Brice has always been at the front of innovative ideas. Think of me as a pilot project," he ordered succinctly.

Max Dragonski tapped his cigar on an ashtray. His gaze returned to Sam's shirt, strolling slowly over it. "Mixing corporate business and private business are two different things, Sam. I agree with the other members. I'm uncomfortable about this."

Relying on instincts that had served him well, Sam made a quick decision. He turned to the windows again, outlining the idea silently and ignoring the hushed snickers behind him. Rubbing his jaw, Sam turned. He knew exactly how to use his height and stare to disintegrate challenging counterparts.

No one snickered about Dallas.

He surveyed the men, then spread his hands on the table and leaned on them. "I'd appreciate your cooperation in this matter. Emily, set up a time that's agreeable with the members, then contact Pendragon to see if she's in sync. Gentlemen of the board, you're welcome to meet Pendragon. She'll be willing to answer any or all questions—I suggest you stick to business."

He paused, trying to ignore Emily's pleased grimace. "Anyone having problems with my place of residence, I'll meet you in my private gym after the meeting. Meeting adjourned—"

At the door, Emily smiled toothily. "Mr. Loring, Ms. Pendragon is just outside. I'm sure she wouldn't mind an interview with the board now."

Knowing Emily's persistence, Sam nodded curtly. "Gentlemen," he said a moment later as Dallas swept into the room, wearing a navy skirt and sweater and carrying a briefcase. "This is our Ms. Pendragon."

Sam noted Dallas's tiny flinch before she smiled coolly at him. Dallas didn't want to be anyone's Ms. Anything, keeping her possession to herself. The thought irritated him mildly. He'd never wanted to fully possess a woman—to wrap himself in her warmth and take care of her. The thought that perhaps he now wanted to, which was as desireable as fleas on a hound dog's back, hurt.

Introducing the board to Dallas, Sam glanced down at
her. Shooting him a quick frown, she glanced at his shirt.
Why was everyone so fascinated with his damned shirt? Her
green eyes darkened and her mouth tightened. "Sam," she
said with quiet force.

"The gentlemen would like to ask you a few questions,
Dallas. Would now be a good time?"

"Sam," she repeated more forcefully, glancing meaningfully at his shoulder.

"Ah, Ms. Pendragon. About this matter of management
providing child-care centers..." a board member began.

"It would cut down on absenteeism when a child is sick
and give the workers time to run down to check on their
children during lunch and breaks," she answered, edging in
front of Sam.

Dallas glanced over her shoulder. "Ah, Mr. Loring,
would you mind sitting down and getting more comfortable?" she asked, tugging out a chair for him.

He shrugged, noting the skill with which she moved into
the spotlight and arranged another meeting for a formal
presentation. Pendragon knew how to pitch, he decided,
watching her field a battery of questions.

"I see this whole thing as a waste of company time—"

"When a company stops trying to improve, I think it
demonstrates a tendency to stagnate, don't you?" Dallas
answered, smiling.

She knew how to throw out challenges, Sam decided,
watching her move around the room in that long-legged
stride. He wondered idly if she were wearing her weekday
panties or the violet splashed ones.

"You don't think you're getting special privileges because of Sam, do you?" Brent Pennington asked slowly.
"He's never allowed anything to interrupt company policy
before—"

Sam tapped his thumb on the wooden arm of the conference chair. Pennington had wanted to show off from the day
he arrived. "Brent—"

Dallas flashed a quick smile at Sam, stopping him from slashing the little punk down to size. She continued the interview in a light, brisk manner while pushing her theories and promising backup statistics. Then not lingering, Dallas discreetly excused herself and gave the members a chance to talk without her presence.

"She's on the ball. Quick thinker," Swearingen said later as he left the room. He grinned at Sam, glancing at his wrinkled shirt. "Better hogtie that one. If I were a few years younger..."

"Sam, I think you're coming along nicely," Emily noted when the room had cleared. "Except you really should learn to use fabric softener in the wash."

Distracted by the depth of his feeling about protecting Dallas, Sam frowned. "What the hell has laundry got to do with a business conference?"

Emily plucked a pink pair of cotton panties from Sam's back. She dropped them on top of his notes and grimaced happily. "Fabric softener stops cling."

She pointed to his shirt front and added, "Take clothes out of the drier ASAP—as soon as possible—and hang them up. I'll take care of Mr. Pennington and his remarks—*I control the switchboard hold button, you know* Until he learns better, his calls will take quite some time to process. On Monday, I'll sneak you some recipes that are good, easy and cheap. Do all the laundry and major grocery shopping during the weekend and leave Sunday night for relaxation... Have a nice weekend."

Sam barely heard her leave as he picked up Dallas's practical underpants, crushing them in his fist. With "Monday" scripted on the cotton, they would be the same pair she'd worn in his office. Sam jammed them into his slacks pocket, the one with Billy's tiny truck, and hoped he had enough saved to pay the baby-sitter.

By the following Friday, Sam felt stretched like a rubberband between his office and household duties. If he had to admit honestly which ones he preferred, he would choose basking in the cheery warmth of the Pendragon household.

At nine o'clock, he settled down to working his way quietly through reports. Emily's voice cutting into his intercom was urgently sharp. "Billy's sick. The sitter couldn't get Ms. Pendragon. Her office says she's on a two-hour trip to a class and can't be reached—"

"I'll go. Cancel all my appointments for the day," Sam ordered, thinking that Billy had been too quiet this morning. His eyes had a weepy look—

"Morrison and Forbes are scheduled for a conference at one, Mr. Loring. They won't talk to anyone but you—"

"Those—" Sam clamped his teeth together and began stashing papers into his briefcase. "The kid is sick, Emily," he said, striding past her on his way to the parking lot. "I'll check in as soon as I see what the situation is."

Sam didn't think about Emily's quiet, pleased smirk; he worried about Billy.

The boy was hot and droopy, too easily managed as Sam carried him into the house. Though the baby-sitter said that Billy's temperature had dropped and that a doctor wasn't necessary, Sam doubted her credentials. But Billy just wanted to be held, snuggling to Sam quietly.

In an hour, Sam had dressed Billy in his Superman pajamas, served him iced orange juice and sat on the couch. Holding the small boy, his blanket, toys and Baghdad on his lap, Sam felt helpless. In his lifetime, he'd worked through rough times, but holding the listless, warm child to him, Sam knew he had never worried so much.

Dozing in his arms, Billy sniffed once and all the muscles in Sam's body tensed. Should he have taken the boy to the emergency room?

"Want macaroni and cheese," Billy mumbled against Sam's chest.

"It's not lunchtime, Billy. How about—"

"Want macaroni and cheese."

The phone rang and Sam extended a hand to retrieve it, muffling a curse. The boy was sick—didn't the world know he couldn't handle macaroni, a sick child and whatever the person on the other end of the line wanted? Forgetting for a moment where he was, he snapped, "Loring here."

Emily spoke in hushed tones. "How's Billy, Mr. Loring?"

"Look, Emily. I'm busy here. I've got my hands full—ouch!" Sam eased Baghdad's kneading claws from his thigh.

"Ah...Mr. Loring? Lisa Pendragon called." Emily smothered a sound that could have been a girlish giggle. "She's picking up Nikki and delivering her to the house. Nikki isn't feeling well. When Ms. Pendragon's office called, I knew you'd need help—"

Knowing that help was on its way, Sam took a relieved breath.

"Mm...cheese...now," Billy mumbled just before he sat up, leaned over and emptied his stomach on Sam's stocking covered foot.

"Call you back—I can make it until Lisa gets here—" Sam said, holding the boy carefully with one hand as he extended his foot and grimaced.

"Sam! Don't hang up!" Emily's imperial shout stopped him from hanging up the receiver.

"What?"

"Lisa Pendragon also said that she's got to catch a flight out right away. She'll drop Nikki by—she said the girl isn't really sick, just something about an upset stomach. She knows you can handle the sick children competently."

Sam felt sick. He knew how the Lone Ranger felt without Tonto. He knew how the captain of the *Titanic* felt. He knew how his foot felt. "Okay," he agreed weakly, then replaced the receiver.

Just after cleaning and changing Billy and himself, Sam reinstated the child on the couch. While he was mixing another batch of orange juice, Lisa delivered Nikki, kissed his cheek and sailed off in her red sports car.

"Glad you're aboard," Sam muttered Lisa's cheerful parting comment.

By the time he settled Nikki comfortably at the other end of the couch, Billy was looking at him with huge, haunting eyes. "Want Mom. Want macaroni and cheese," he demanded softly in a hurt tone, as if Sam were sloughing off his duties.

At one o'clock in the afternoon, Sam was exhausted. The house looked like a tornado had passed through, and the phone rang again. Emily asked, "How are they doing, Mr. Loring?"

"Sleeping," he whispered back, removing two dolls and three tiny trucks from the couch. "What's up?"

"Morrison and Forbes are in your office, ready for a conference call. Can you handle it?"

Rolling his eyes upward for heavenly help, Sam agreed. Sitting on the floor with his briefcase opened, he conducted an entire business deal in whispers.

Sometime between two and three—between Nikki's request for juice and Billy's for a story—Sam dozed, stretched out on the floor beside the couch. He was exhausted, worried and . . . exhausted.

The phone rang, and he snatched it instantly. "Sam?" Dallas asked softly. "I just got the message—but Emily said you had everything under control. I'm sorry I wasn't there, but I'm driving back as soon as I can. Thanks, Sam," she added hesitantly.

"The kids are okay," Sam whispered. "They're better now. They're both sleeping and don't have a temperature. It's like the sitter said, just a passing thing."

"I have a girlfriend who comes over at times like this. If you need to get back to the office, I'll call her—"

"Not a chance. I've got everything under control," Sam whispered, glancing around the house. If he hurried, he could just clean up before she arrived and make the whole day look like a walk through the park.

In the next ten minutes, just as Sam slipped back into comfortable dozing, someone knocked at the front door.

When he opened it, Emily grinned and held out papers to him. "You have to sign these today, Mr. Loring."

Glancing at the papers, Sam scrawled his signature, took another look and wiped away a crumb of the Sunbirds' Cookies. Emily vanished before he could ask her to help him clean up.

After another frantic two hours, Sam managed to clean the house, wash the soiled clothing, fix peanut-butter sandwiches and read a story to the children.

When Dallas arrived, opening the door quietly, Sam dozed on the floor. He blinked at her as she bent over him and smoothed his hair.

"Poor Sam," she said in the sweet, hushed tones he loved to hear. He blinked again, trying to look as though the experience was something he could easily manage. But he'd lost a whole day somehow and he had paperwork to finish for a contract discussion he had rescheduled for the morning.

"Hi, Mommy," Billy said brightly, stepping over Sam's prone body. "I was sick, but Mr. Sam took care of me and now I feel great! Want to play, Mr. Sam?"

"Hi, Mom," Nikki chimed in, evidently recovered. "What's wrong with Sam? Why's he just laying there staring up at the ceiling like that?"

Seven

Monday morning, Sam threw his briefcase onto his desk. Dallas had spent the better part of the weekend at her office or in her bedroom plotting his downfall. In the three weeks since he'd met her, he'd had nothing but trouble.

He jammed his fists into his jeans pockets, resenting that he had shot Rule 2.01 of Brice's Executive Dress Code to hell. He didn't have the money for dry cleaning the suits splattered with Bertha's oil patterns. It was the first time in his ten years at Brice that he had worn a sweater over a wash-and-wear shirt.

Running a hand along his collar, he grimaced. The longish length of his hair—also because of temporary budgetary problems—was a blatant infraction of Rule 2.02.

Nikki had forgotten her favorite doll, and Billy's zipper had stuck, causing Sam to be late to the office, thus breaking Brice's rule for prompt business hours.

Sam extended a long leg, checking the length of the jeans to see if it covered the new bleach spots on his dress socks. He'd lost the appropriate mates and had found an odd assortment clinging to everything, haunting him. Dallas hoarded her clothes, and he doubted that he could handle them without hormonal distress. The thoughts of her monogrammed panties had kept him from reworking a market report due in January.

Rubbing his hand along his jaw, Sam admitted that playing working parent and house husband wasn't as easy as it had first appeared.

He'd never wanted children, but he'd miss Nikki and Billy. His past Christmas seasons seemed empty now that he'd experienced the warmth and excitement of children. While other children seemed to want enormous lists from Santa Claus, Nikki and Billy just wanted Mr. Sam.

He explored the novelty of being wanted for himself and decided it hadn't happened in his lifetime.

Someone always wanted something from him—work, money, gifts. And he'd given and taken without any remorse or lingering attachments.

Sam rubbed his hands together, chafing away the cold he felt seeping into his life.

Living with Dallas wasn't easy. Her scents filled the house; her laughter caused his breathing to change.

Thoughts of her aching little sighs had kept him from sleeping. Dallas was working too hard, looking bleak and hollow eyed. He thought of her savage, hungry expression as she lay in his arms...her body arching toward his touch...and then Sam groaned. He didn't want to step into commitments at his age, much less a relationship. Especially with a woman who was his enemy in business, proposing weird ideas about stress management.

Were they weird? he wondered, acknowledging the tension he felt trying to balance his new home life and a business. And why hadn't he some idea that his employees were unhappy before Dallas started turning over policies?

Okay, he'd been busy, fighting to keep Brice at the top and concerned about production. Of course, he cared, it was just that he had no idea—

Just as Dallas had no idea of her sensuality until lately. She'd be a man's living dream—a lady in public and responsive in bed.

Surf-boy Mullens would be waiting for her to fall into his bed. Or would Beau, the wimp, taste those strawberry lips?

Scowling at the fog bank encompassing his office, Sam noted the colored holiday lights below his office. Christmas was next week, the children were excited and he had empty pockets.

For a reason Sam didn't want to explore, he needed to give Dallas something special. A part of himself.

When was the last time he'd wanted to share any part of himself with anyone? Sam wondered.

When was the last time he'd shared the warmth of a real home, felt children snuggle against him after a really good round of bear hunting—

He caught the scent of coffee—an extravagance he couldn't afford—and turned around to see Emily placing a cup of delicious, steaming brew on his desk. "Bless you," he murmured humbly, inhaling the scent and cupping the warm cup in his hands.

She placed a folder stuffed with odd papers on his desk as he sipped the coffee. "Recipes from the staff. They're enjoying your trials as a working mother, you know. One of them said that you were almost human. Especially when you're mooning over that Pendragon woman. They think you should take her on a date, maybe dinner overlooking the bay."

Sam stopped sipping, stretching Emily's charity. "With what?"

"Limits one, doesn't it?" she asked cheerfully. "Don't forget. The gifts for the office party and donations to the needy are expected of you, like everyone else. I can't write your charity check this year," she added with a tiny drop of humor. "But, of course, I can see that the accounting branch prepares the Christmas bonuses, if you wish. Oh, and Ms. Pendragon will be here at ten for a conference with you. She has questions that need clearance before she can proceed. Mr. Mullens will be with her, the lovely man.''

Emily glanced at Sam's dark expression, then winked, and before leaving his office, she added, ''Lisa called. She and Edward Swearingen have been seeing each other. They're taking the children for the weekend. Sledding and marshmallow roasts at his cabin on Snoqualmie Pass. You and Ms. Pendragon will just have to make do this weekend. Alone.''

Alone. The word stopped Sam in midswallow. Dallas would be his for the weekend. *No children. No Lisa.* Sam swallowed, wondering why he felt so light-headed.

Between calls and dictation, Sam worked on his plans for the weekend alone with Dallas...candlelight dinners, low lights and Crab Louie, Seattle's famous seafood salad. Or maybe he should take her to dinner and dancing at the bay. Sam mentally rummaged through his wallet and wondered if Emily knew any romantic ''stretcher'' meals.

When Dallas arrived for her ten o'clock conference, she spread the first-floor plan across Sam's desk and pointed at it. ''This would be the best spot for a child-care center. Employees could easily drop the children off when they arrive and pick them up when they leave. That floor is also the best place to put a gym and shower system. However, if you think another spot would be appropriate, we can estimate that, too. Can't we, Carl?''

She glanced up to find Carl Mullens and Sam glaring at each other over her head. While Carl's expression was bland, Sam's dark eyebrows were jammed together, his jaw rigid. They looked like two alley toms snarling over territorial rights. Dressed in a woolen ski sweater and jeans, Sam appeared rugged and appealing next to Carl's polished carelessness.

''Ah...Carl, would you mind going on without me?'' Dallas touched his arm and felt Sam tensing at her side.

"Sure thing, baby," Carl mumbled, shooting one last hard look at Sam before walking his tight jeans out of the office.

"Sure thing, baby," Sam repeated through his teeth as he glanced at her navy, pin-striped chemise dress. "Is that jerk really any good?"

Something went fluttering about in her when Sam's hard stare lingered on her mouth. He looked so grim, she couldn't resist teasing him a little. "At what?"

Watching her, Sam slowly removed his glasses and placed them on the blueprints. "I could show you what," he returned in that low Southern drawl, reaching for her.

She stepped back. For a moment they just looked at each other, breathing hard. Sam did look delicious. Wickedly masculine and sexy. There was something primitive roaming around within him, as if he wanted her more than anything in his life.

Dallas lowered her eyelids, feeling her cheeks warm. Sam's large hand cupped her chin, lifting it as he smiled tenderly. "You're blushing, Ms. Businesswoman of the Year."

When he brushed his lips across her cheek, Dallas couldn't force herself to move away. She breathed quietly, trying to sort out the emotions within her. "Shoo," she ordered weakly as he drew away.

"Are you wearing your Monday panties, Ms. Pendragon?" Sam's deep sexy drawl reached right inside her. His intercom buzzed, and Sam jabbed a button on it, clearly irritated by the interruption. "What?"

"Call on line two from Nikki and Billy," Emily crooned softly.

Holding Dallas's worried gaze, Sam took the call. "Hi, you mean, tough bear hunters."

He nodded, watching Dallas. "I know, Nikki. You're right, your doll does need a bigger crib—one that rocks. Okay, Billy, we'll go down to the mall to see Santa Claus. Uh-huh, I do have a present for your mother," he said, beginning to smile.

Sam slipped his hand around hers, his thumb caressing Dallas's knuckles as he listened to the children intently. Dallas stood quietly, absorbing the gentle strength in the same hand that ruled Brice Cleansers and dressed Nikki's dolls. Then for a moment, his thumb stilled and Sam frowned, apparently listening closely. "Thank you," he said quietly, his voice raspy. "It will be the best one I've ever had. Okay. And let's stop on the way home for ice-cream cones to celebrate, okay? You want to talk to your mother? She's right here—"

Big, tough Sam Loring definitely looked weak and pale as he sprawled into a chair. He stared off into space while the receiver dangled from his limp hand.

Taking the telephone, Dallas learned that the baby-sitter wanted a new kitchen sponge for Christmas. When she placed the telephone in the cradle, she asked, "Sam? What's wrong?"

He stared at her blankly, and she caught the damp glitter on his lashes before he lowered his head to study the plans. When his shoulders tensed, Dallas placed her hand on his arm. Sam's muscles contracted beneath the woolen sweater. He rotated his neck as though it ached, and Dallas instinctively began rubbing the taut muscles.

Taking her hand in his, Sam raised her palm to his mouth. She allowed the intimacy because Sam looked so helpless. "Billy just called me 'Daddy,'" he managed to say unevenly against her skin. He breathed deeply. "Daddy," Sam repeated reverently. "And they're making me a stocking. God, I'm forty-six—"

"Don't let it go to your head, big guy," Dallas said softly, smoothing his hair. She'd advised Billy about the "don't-call-Sam-Daddy" matter, but apparently her son had slipped in a wayward moment.

She liked how the crisp texture of Sam's hair clung to her skin and enjoyed petting Sam in his moment of weakness. Normally he was so solid and impending, the thought of soothing him was like reaching her hand into a tiger's lair.

Because he was so vulnerable, because she was so frightened of caring again, Dallas stepped away. She rummaged through her large purse, extracted a paper bag and tossed it to him. "I brought you a present."

Opening the bag carefully, Sam shook the contents onto his desk. A Kaiser bun stuffed with alfalfa sprouts, sliced tomato and assorted lunch meats in plastic wrap looked delicious. Dallas handed him a small thermos, the scent of clam chowder filling the room when he opened it. "I know you've been skipping lunches by the way you stock up at night. This might help."

He looked astonished and very uneasy. He swallowed, and his mouth worked a fraction of time before he actually spoke. "This is very nice," Sam said stiffly, then cleared his throat.

Poor Sam, Dallas thought, watching him stare at the sandwich and hot soup. He swallowed again. "I haven't brown bagged it in fifteen years or more," he said in a deep, uneven voice. "Thanks."

Because Sam was so clearly touched, Dallas couldn't resist bending to kiss his cheek. Then his mouth turned slightly, and she stood still as Sam's lips worshipped hers, tasting and warming.

Though his hands didn't touch her, she was drawn nearer by the soft, cherishing movements of his mouth. Dallas found herself leaning into his warmth, resting against the strength of his body while Sam slanted his mouth to nibble at her bottom lip. "I've missed you, sweet pea," he said huskily against her chin, easing her gently into his lap. "Come here."

Resting her hand on his chest, Dallas looked up at his tender expression and traced a new shaving cut. "Don't mess with me, Sam," she returned shakily. "I'm really not up to any of this."

He smiled at that, nibbling on the tip of her finger and gently sucking it. "What makes you think I am?"

"You're not what I want." Why were his eyes so tender? Why did she feel so safe in his arms?

Why couldn't he have been anyone else? Someone less demanding, like Beau or Doug...?

"I haven't wanted anyone for years," he said as though to himself.

"Then don't want me," she returned, raising her lips for his kiss.

The instant their lips met, Dallas forgot to resist. She forgot to keep Sam in the T.J. category of women-using men and allowed herself to listen to the throbbing jungle drums. Running her hand behind his head, she toyed with the crisp, longish hair at his collar.

When his tongue flicked lightly at the corners of her mouth, Dallas parted her lips and drew him nearer. She wanted his mouth desperately, wanted the heat and strength of Sam wrapped nearer about her. Under her, over her—

"Sam?" Dallas needed to press her mouth against the rough skin covering that throbbing vein. When she did, the jungle tom-toms began beating rapidly, unevenly.

Moving deeper into Sam's arms, Dallas forgot everything but the way he tasted. She explored his lips with her tongue, listened to his quiet, uneven breathing as she tugged at his sweater, lifting it upward and over his head.

Fighting the heat moving through her, Dallas sat straighter and studied the way his hair stood up in peaks. The way his hard mouth had softened with her kiss. He tasted wonderful. Like tender promises and warm Southern nights scented by magnolia blossoms.

She loved the way he trembled, the heat flushing his cheeks, and the stormy gray color of his eyes. On her hip, his hand trembled, and Dallas suddenly wanted it on her, roaming, searching and finding.

Delighted in a way she had never been, Dallas reached down to grip Sam's shirt in both hands. The buttons tore easily, popping off with little, exciting snaps.

Like her taut, feminine senses.

Beneath the stained and wrinkled—but clean—shirt, Sam's chest and throat were wonderful. Exciting and waiting to be discovered like a sumptuous new dessert. Rubbing her nose against Sam's soap-scented, hair-covered muscular chest, Dallas wanted to be near him. Laminated to him.

Winding her arms around his neck, she drew him down for her kiss. Breathing rapidly, Sam tightened his arms, his large hands warming her back and hips and legs. He was moving too slowly when Dallas's tom-toms weren't waiting—too gently when she wanted him hot and close.

"Sam-boy?" she asked huskily against his cheek, feeling the underlying heat as he trembled.

"Ouch," he muttered as her hips shifted more comfortably within his hard lap. Lifting her easily with one arm, Sam extracted a tiny toy truck and a frilly doll dress to carefully place them on the desk.

He grinned with the air of a boy savoring a double-dipped chocolate ice-cream cone. "Now where were we?"

Dallas fought the heat building within her, fought the tender look of expectancy on Sam's dark face. With his hair mussed by her fingers, his eyes dark and wickedly pleased, Sam was too masculine, too enticing, too—

His bottom lip was cut, and she stared at it blankly.

Holding very still beneath her, Sam watched her closely. "You bit me, sweet pea," he said in a deep, ragged tone that reminded her of spreading a blanket beneath the stars. Near a lily pond with frogs and crickets. "And called me Sam-boy. Did wonders for my ego."

Dallas's eyes widened, meeting the dark humor in his. "Me?" She managed in a tone that sounded like a squeak.

"You." Sam kissed her sensitive mouth lightly. Then he grinned, looking down at his bare chest and her undisturbed clothing. "Sorry to take advantage of you this way," he drawled in his sexiest Southern accents. "But I just couldn't help myself."

Throughout the week, Dallas fought cost estimates, ran her business through her assistants and suffered from a lack of sleep due to hearing Sam move about in the basement . . . and his sweet kiss. Dallas had heard her tom-toms every night, awakening to find herself twisted in rosebud sheets and aching with the empty promise of her dreams.

The Deons were on a sizzling, kissing rampage everywhere she looked.

Sam made coffee every morning, dressed in loose pajama bottoms. They were originally white, but assorted pinks and blues had stained the cotton. She found herself thinking how easily that knot at his enticing navel could be tugged loose. . . .

Even after she reminded them that Sam's stay was only temporary, Nikki and Billy were calling the squatter and usurper of her hormones Daddy. Each time they did, Sam reacted in a humble, loveable way that caused her to forget her mission for a moment.

Nothing about Sam was safe, at least what parts touched her. Every morning when she had handed Sam his lunch, he'd stared down at her in that quiet way that said he knew something she didn't.

She loved handing Sam his lunch. He took it with such reverence and appreciation, as though each time was a brand-new gift that he hadn't expected.

She had scheduled a date with Beau on Friday evening. She'd badly needed a kiss to compare with Sam's unholy devastation. When Beau had come to pick her up, Sam had seemed in unusually good humor, clapping Beau on the back. "Have fun, kids. I won't wait up," he had said, returning to the contents of his briefcase beneath the snickerdoodle cookie recipes.

Beau had shuddered openly. Later—after Sam's kiss—Dallas had shuddered, too.

Without the children to consider, Sam went on a midnight binge of sawing, hammering gently and making a spine-tingling scrape-scrape she recognized as sanding.

Dallas ran cost estimates of labor for a child-care center, sniffed the new potpourri Sam had added to the simmering pot, and wondered why T.J.'s kiss hadn't moved her to tearing off his clothes.

Pulling her rosebud-splattered sheets over her head, Dallas tried to ignore the disturbing creature in her basement.

She couldn't trust Sam Loring for a moment. He was sneaky, waiting for a chance to shoot holes in her presentation. Waiting for a time when he could get her beneath his thumb and spread her failure as a woman before the world.

She was a failure in bed. Hadn't T.J. told her often enough?

Why hadn't she kept herself safe? What she'd actually done by instigating Lisa's scheme was to place the fox in the hen house. The saw buzzed merrily in the basement shop, and Dallas forced herself not to grit her teeth.

Loring was cunning. With her senses running wild and his saws buzzing all night, she couldn't possibly put together a decent proposal.

With that thought, she sat upright, turning on her bedside light. Loring's kisses and sawing wouldn't keep her from designing the best proposal the Seattle business world had ever experienced. Dragging her briefcase into the bed with her, Dallas began jotting down notes on a legal pad. If he could work all night, so could she. Dallas spritzed herself with cool rosewater she kept beside her bed, breathed deeply and began working on The Whammy Plan Designed for Business Executives.

The Whammy, a working plan to educate managers, needed refining. The Whammy would demonstrate employee stresses created by managerial demands. It involved inverted cross-training, where managers sat at a secretarial desk and performed light clerical duties. Dallas smiled as she jotted down her notes. She doubted if Sam could fit his long legs under a secretarial desk. Let alone tactfully settle office disputes before they got out of hand.

Saturday morning she awoke to the sound of hammering in the basement. Dragging herself into the shower, then dressing in jeans and sweatshirt, Dallas left the house for her office. She intended to push the proposal into shape for the January consideration by Brice's board. By making good use of the weekend, she could enjoy Christmas with her family.

During the day, she found herself thinking of Sam.

It wasn't often a woman found a man who preferred boxer shorts to the newer bikini cut. Before Sam discovered fabric softener, his cotton shorts clung to towels and sheets, which had been folded with methodical precision. She missed finding the assortment of underwear, she admitted reluctantly.

T.J. had preferred minuscule black shorts cut across his hips for vanity's sake. Sam, on the other hand, didn't have an ounce of vanity in his hard muscular frame. He had scarred knuckles and a neck that seemed to lower into his shoulders when he was angry. He had big, gentle hands that dressed dolls and felt warm and safe when they caressed her skin—

Dallas closed her eyes and shivered. It had to be the Christmas season or midlife approaching. In the afternoon, Sybil dropped in with a thermos of seasonal cheer. She vaguely mentioned something about rum.

At five o'clock, Dallas found herself exiting her computer outline. Deeply tired and drained, she hadn't made progress for the past hour and recognized her problem easily. As a businesswoman, she couldn't afford distraction and knew she had better deal with it.

The game plan had shifted, and Sam presented an immense, personal problem to her. Driving through the cold drizzle, Dallas worked out a tentative plan to let Sam out of his part of the contract. She nodded to the swish-swish of her windshield wipers. Sam could move back into his penthouse and they'd modify his life-style from there.

Parking over Bertha's new pool of oil, Dallas smiled. Sam would buy the wager's modification and move out. Given some space, she could erase the hot, tight feeling when he pulled out his damned dimples and Southern drawl.

Feeling in control for the first time in weeks, Dallas walked up the steps and opened the door with new confidence.

Sam, seated on the living-room floor and surrounded by wrapping paper and wooden toys, glowered up at her. Particles of sawdust clung to his longish hair. A peek-a-boo hole in his T-shirt exposed a nipple circled by hair, and his muscular legs were bare from his pink boxer shorts to his mismatched socks. The scent of spaghetti and garlic bread mixed with winter-pine potpourri swirled around her as she studied him—the villain who kept crashing uninvited into her outline for the Brice proposal.

Sam's neck began to sink into his broad shoulders in a gesture she now recognized as self-defense.

He flexed his fingers—the ones trapped in cellophane tape. "I was going to clean up and have supper waiting—spaghetti. Barbara in accounting gave me the recipe for sauce. You *said* you'd call before you came home," he accused between his teeth.

"Darned if I didn't," she agreed lightly, trying to ignore the skipping of her heart.

Noting the mistletoe ball just directly over his head, Dallas longed to taste his mouth....

He rubbed his unshaven cheek against his shoulder, dislodging a scrap of wrapping paper with a smiling Santa Claus on it. "It's Christmas," he growled in his grumpy bear-in-the-cave tone. "Get lost."

Sam deserved a little irritating for creeping into her computer outline repeatedly. Dallas kicked off her canvas shoes, threw her jacket onto the couch and curled into one corner. Feeling warm and cozy, she spread herself luxuriously over the cabbage roses. "Nikki will love the doll crib," she said, meaning it as she studied the handcrafted toy. Little hearts decorated the little rocking crib. A box with a leather latch had Billy's name stenciled on it. "Billy needed a toy box."

"It's a box for special things," Sam informed her in an arrogant sniff. "Has compartments and drawers for keeper items. Every boy needs one."

"What did you make me, Sam?" she asked, enjoying the way he flexed his fingers within the masses of tape.

"I'm not telling," he returned, lowering his eyebrows at her as a muscle contracted in his cheek. "I thought I told you to beat it. Go back to the office and call me. Drive carefully—the streets are slick.''

"You're not handing out orders, are you?" she asked, prodding him and knowing it. When Sam's neck sunk lower into his shoulders and he glared at her from beneath the thick line of his eyebrows, she teased, "You're a cellophane-tape prisoner."

Tilting her head, Dallas asked speculatively, "I wonder if Mr. Sam Loring, business hardhead, is ticklish."

Sam stared at her, his gray eyes stormy. "I don't know what's wrong with you . . . but touch me, Pendragon, and I won't be responsible."

"Tired from all that midnight sawing, are we?" she asked, kneeling down to face him. Looking disgruntled and yet rawly masculine, Sam sat there looking like her special Christmas package from Santa Claus.

"Tired enough to know that you and I are alone in the house for the first time. Tired enough to know that if you don't control your . . . impulses to torment me, I just might do something rash. And I've been the perfect gentleman so far," he muttered, seeking the end of the tape with his teeth and jerking it. "I've got aches to prove it."

"Oh, yeah?" she asked, heady with a breathless erotic power she'd never experienced. The thoughts of having Sam, helpless and sexy, within her touch went to her head like a rum drink.

She never touched drinks with rum in them—except for this afternoon. Once, after a rum drink, she'd danced a flamenco on a table. With the Christmas-tree lights twinkling above her, she placed her arms around Sam's neck as he watched her warily. "What are you up to?"

Dallas glanced upward at the mistletoe ball and Sam's gaze followed hers. "Trust me," Dallas urged against his mouth, needing the taste of him.

As she leaned into him, Sam swayed backward, crushing the wrapping paper beneath him. Pressuring him just a little more, Dallas forced him to the floor.

"I'm not easy," Sam said unevenly, the reindeer-and-Christmas-tree paper rustling beneath his head.

But Dallas was listening to the beat of her special tom-toms and fitted herself over him. She'd never wanted to be touched so badly in her life. She was cold and lonely while the Deons were hoarding all the heat. Midlife was waiting like a big, black chilling hole, and she wanted a memory to take with her into the abyss. She needed the heat in Sam flowing over her as it had behind his desk that day. She'd shuttled through the rocky relationship with T.J. only to discover her dreams were shattered.

A kiss from Douglas hadn't caused a ripple of heat. And Beau just couldn't manage a kiss.

But Sam knew how to make her feel as though she were desired. A very feminine, desirable woman.

When Sam walked away, she would deal with the ache. But later—

"Shoo," he ordered huskily as she nibbled at the delectable corner of his mouth. He hadn't shaved, and the rough texture of his new beard sent a fresh wave of longing over her. She stroked his taut cheeks, soothing Sam as she had wanted to from the beginning.

She could feel the ache and the loneliness of his life spread into her. Taking her time, Dallas traced his features with her fingertips and followed their trail.

Somehow Sam's hands were free then, and he was touching her, moving her beneath him and crushing the reindeer wrapping paper. Along her cheeks, his rough fingers were trembling and warm. Keeping the heavy weight of his body from her, Sam stroked her hair back from her cheeks. "Don't mess with the cook," he murmured softly, looking down at her.

Holding his dark gaze, Dallas allowed her fingers to prowl downward. They found the peek-a-boo hole and slid through it to toy with his nipple. Over her, Sam's taut body hardened as she circled the flat nub. "You're asking for it, sweet pea," he threatened in a low, Southern drawl accented with dimples.

"Oh, Sam," she murmured helplessly as he eased away from her. "Oh, Sam," she repeated uncertainly as he picked her up and carried her into her bedroom.

Eight

"Sam," she whispered a third time as he gently placed her on her bed.

In the shadows of the room, Sam stood looking down at her, his hands placed on his waist. Then he turned slowly and walked out of the room, closing the door and leaving her alone in the dark with the rosebuds.

She suddenly heard the shower running and she wanted to cry. Aching with a cold space inside her, Dallas forced herself to strip and slip into her flannel nightgown. She eased beneath the blankets with the feeling of being very old and unwanted.

Curling into a ball and turning on her side, she drew the quilt higher and fought the cold. With the children and her career keeping her busy, she'd been successful at forgetting.... Looking into the darkness beyond the window, she knew why Sam had left her alone.

You can't keep a man turned on, baby, T.J. muttered through the distance of the years.

Then the door opened, the hallway light slicing through T.J.'s demeaning growl. Outlined there, Sam's body looked tall and dangerous.

Dressed in his shorts, Sam balanced a tray filled with a teapot and a cup-and-saucer. "You need this," he said softly, crossing into the darkness with her and shutting the door.

Placing the tray on her bedside table, Sam poured tea. Taking the saucer from him, Dallas sipped the hot liquid slowly. She averted her head, not wanting Sam to see the tears chilling her cheeks.

"Scoot over," he ordered mildly, lifting the covers to slide into the bed with her.

"Shoo," she muttered unevenly, trying not to sniff. She didn't want him meddling in her private pain, searching out the weaknesses and the scars. "Go away."

"Not a chance, Pendragon." Sam's deep voice was smooth Southern honey covering the business steel—his trademark. Propping the pillows up behind him, he placed his arm around her and eased her against his side. "You *are* a virus. When I moved in here I thought I'd give you a dose of your own medicine. You've gotten under my skin and you're driving me nuts," he admitted roughly against her temple. "Maybe I should get you out of my system. If I can."

When she tried to ease away from the temptation of his warm body, knowing that she couldn't afford another dismissal à la T.J., Sam's arm held her tightly against him. He'd skim away her defenses and see everything, she thought desperately, trying to escape his warm thigh pressed up against hers. He'd see how inadequate she was.

Sam rocked her gently at his side, wriggling his toes against her cold ones. "Nice, isn't it? Two old folks snuggling in a four-poster bed while the kids are at Grandma's," he said, wry humor tinting his deep, lazy drawl. "You're even wearing a flannel nighty."

His fingers caressed her arm slowly. "Shoo," she repeated without force, knowing that if he did go she'd wither in the cold, barren loneliness.

"Hush," he murmured against her ear, taking the saucer from her to place it on the bedside table. "Feeling better? Or are you still feeling amorous because of the rum?"

"Amorous? Rum?" She tried unsuccessfully for an innocent tone, tinged with a pinch of indignation.

When she turned to stare at him, Sam kissed her lightly. "Honey, you tasted like it. And your mother told me you're primitive if you have a drop. What I want to know is, how do you explain yourself without it . . . ?"

He began unbuttoning her gown, lowering his head to taste the soft skin he uncovered. With his lips against her, Sam asked, "Do you know what you're doing, sweet pea?"

She swallowed, trembling as she tried to resist touching him. It was a moment for truth, and she'd have to deal with the aftermath later. The honorable thing to do, of course, was to prepare him for her lack of skill. "Yes, I know," she found herself whispering helplessly.

Poor man, she thought sadly. Nestled so sexily against her, his muscular legs tangling with her flannel-covered ones, Sam would be so disappointed.

Sam's mouth found the tip of her breast, his teeth toying with it gently as he unbuttoned her gown down to her ankles. "Do you want me, sweet pea?" he asked.

"Yesss," she said shakily as Sam stripped the gown from her. If she ever needed anyone, it was Sam. He made her feel magnolia sweet and as lickable as sugar cane. Beneath his touch, she felt dainty and feminine, almost desirable. When he shifted over her, she discovered his shorts were missing.

She began shivering, his hair-roughened body nudging and weighing down hers. Absorbing his heat, adjusting to the hard planes and angles, Dallas felt the first timid beat of a distant tom-tom. She ached to rub herself against the roughness brushing her, arch her thighs against the hardness of his—

Resting lightly on her, Sam kissed her throat. The scent of his soap and after-shave blended with a deeper, intimate musk. Dallas fought exposing her inadequacies. She curled her hands against her thighs with the need to keep from touching him. Against her throat, Sam smiled. "Like I said, a man likes to be touched."

Aching with the need to obey, Dallas forced herself not to notice how touchable Sam was. She wanted to explore him from head to foot—but then he'd see....

She was turning into liquid heat, the jungle drums throbbing rhythmically, coming closer....

Were those her moans blending with the drums?

Someone in that same distance was breathing unevenly as though in a jungle fever.

But she wouldn't touch him. She'd keep her pride intact—what little remained....

Caressing her body with his, Sam nibbled on her ear as his hands moved over her, stroking. When his tongue gently slid into her ear, Dallas gasped as the tom-tom beat quickly. "Oh, Sam," she exclaimed unevenly as he pressed against her.

He kissed a trail to her lips, running his rough palm along her ribs. He molded the curve of her waist as though imprinting it in his memory. His thumb found her navel, circling and pressing it lightly. "How long has it been?"

Looking up at his tense expression, Dallas felt his shudder against the length of her body. Sam wanted her badly, his large body taut with desire. Pressing against her lower stomach, Sam's bold shape both frightened and excited her. A funny little constriction quivered deep within her, waiting. Startled, Dallas tried to push the intimate nudging of her body aside. The stubborn little quiver repeated itself, bringing with it a frightening memory. She didn't want Sam stripping her, finding the cold inside. "It's been years, Sam . . . I can't."

Gently, he nudged her knees apart to fit snugly within her thighs. Sam stroked her cheeks with his thumbs, deepening the intimacy as he looked down at her through the shadows. "You're shaking, Dallas."

Dallas fought the emotions tugging at her. And she fought wanting Sam. "Shoo," she ordered faintly, her palms finding his taut, muscular back.

Smiling softly above her, Sam eased his mouth over hers and kissed her with the most adoring kiss she had ever experienced. "Shoo, yourself," he repeated against her lips.

Shuddering with passion barely controlled, Dallas gasped. "Oh, Sam . . . I'm so afraid." His weight and desire frightened her badly now as she remembered the shafting pain.

Arching against his invasion, Dallas whimpered, trying to withdraw. "God, Dallas, what's wrong?" Sam asked roughly, holding himself taut above her. His thumb rubbed a fresh tear from her cheek.

"Sam, I . . . You . . . This is really a mistake," Dallas began shakily, trembling. Wanting to move into his warmth and fearing the consequences.

"Damned if it is," he muttered, drawing away slightly. Dark, primitive anger swirled inside him, his large body shaking with it. When he scowled, moving as if to leave her, Dallas poised on the brink of her choices—alone, or sharing the heat of passion with this gentle man.

She'd been alone and cold as the drizzling rain beyond the window's lacy curtains. Once after . . . well, after Sam uncovered her faults, she'd be alone again.

She arched her hips slightly, cradling him, keeping him locked closer to her.

Tensed above her, Sam shot her a hot look. "Look, Dallas. Don't mess with me now—I'm trying to give you some space." His voice caught as her hands slid across the hard, hair-covered planes of his chest. "I can understand..." His voice trailed off when her insoles prowled his bulky calves.

The movement brought him slightly into her, and the funny little constrictions began partying.

When he groaned wistfully, the sound slid warmly within her. For now, Sam wanted her. Yet he cared enough to consider her needs, too. She smiled and stroked the nape of his damp neck. Sam was just that sort of guy—gentle, careful, sweet, loveable, and tasty. Even when he made his disgruntled bear noises, she knew he'd never hurt her.

"Come here," she murmured, drawing his head down to hers. "Come here," she repeated, sliding a hand down his back to press his hips against hers.

"Dallas...." He protested because of her obvious fears, and that endeared this rough, gentle man to her. Feeling herself open to him, giving him the warmth he badly needed, Dallas watched him intently.

Sam held himself from her, his expression taut with agony she barely understood. "You have to loosen up, Sam," she teased against his damp throat, feeling herself relax slightly. For a moment, the funny little constrictions paused and wondered.

Sliding her hand downward, wanting to explore...she touched him.

Sam almost leaped out of her arms. "Watch it, Pendragon," he rapped out when he settled uneasily. His mouth slowly curved into a wicked grin that she found herself returning. "This isn't exactly an everyday experience for me, either."

"No?" she asked, repeating the maneuver just to feel his heartbeat pound rapidly against her hot cheek. His admission activated ideas about tying Sam to her four-poster bed and keeping him there until the tom-toms faded and the constrictions were pacified.

"Hell, no," he muttered roughly, easing into her again. His breath caught and his eyes closed when he rested within the tight passage. Sam's broad chest rose and fell unevenly; his lean cheeks were beginning to flush. Beside her, his large hands grasped her pillows, the cords on his arms standing out in relief. "I've been saving myself."

"Well, then..." She ran her fingers through the hair on his chest, prowling through it and then down to his buttocks. She touched his flat stomach, and Sam inhaled sharply.

While she knew Sam was being the perfect Southern gentleman, tender and understanding, Dallas wanted to be untethered and primitively wild.

Sam was so solid and strong, she knew he would keep them both safe as she merrily chartered hot, steamy, unknown jungles. She glanced at Sam's expression and found it so intent, she knew he would take whatever she gave and give it back to her with tender beauty.

Snuggling her hips side to side against his, Dallas found herself adjusting to Sam, who now seemed to have difficulty breathing. He didn't seem to mind as she raised her arms and legs, locking him to her with all her strength.

He held absolutely still while Dallas allowed her fingers to roam across the slightly damp, tense ridges of his back, soothing him. Her teeth found his earlobe, testing it gently. She closed her eyes, luxuriating in the hard, warm, safe feel of Sam at her disposal. She ran her fingers down his shoulder blades and his spine to seek the hollows at the base.

She lifted her hips higher, drawing him even deeper. The hot, riveting constricting, pleasure-pain waves came suddenly, spreading throughout her. Surprised by the pinpointing pleasure deep within, Dallas held Sam with all her strength, knowing that he could keep her safe. His uneven breath swirled about her as the heat rose, consuming her. He trembled as the aftershocks forced her to cry out with pleasure.

"Better?" he asked gently, soothing her breasts with his hands as she drifted through the satiny warmth back to him.

Shaking, powerless against her emotions, Dallas realized how she had acted—fierce, dominating, hungry. Setting the pace was a man's choice, wasn't it? "Oh, no," she groaned softly.

"Oh, yes." Sam caressed her hips, filling his hands with the softness as he raised her to him again. His mouth found her breasts, gently testing the sensitive flesh with his teeth. When he tugged at the peaks, the hunger came raging back full force, her body tightening around him as though it had been starved for an eternity.

A new set of aftershocks shot through her, startling her.

"My turn." Sam reached downward, touching her gently.

Dallas breathed lightly, afraid to move, wrapping herself in the utter pleasure of Sam making love to her.

She closed her eyes as he explored the taut muscles of her throat and shoulders. He tasted her slowly, as though she delighted him and he wanted to savor every inch.

She felt the sweat slick between them, waited for his revulsion, which never came. Sam licked the tip of her breast, tasting it. Experimenting with the sensation of lingering, of enjoying lovemaking, Dallas flicked her tongue along Sam's damp shoulder.

She smiled then, tasting the tang of the salt and the desire between them. Experimenting again, Dallas drew him deeper into her arms. Sam's heart thudded heavily, rapidly against her sensitized breasts. Closing her eyes again, Dallas absorbed Sam into her, unknowingly tightening and tugging him deeper within her body.

She cried out again as he held her tighter. And then there was no time, nothing but the surging joy of Sam and her flying through an endless, silky rainbow.

He held her there, poised delicately within the fire and the pleasure. She ached as she strained for an undefined goal. With a soft cry, Dallas unleased the heat within her, trusting Sam to keep them both safe.

She awoke to Sam's head resting on her breast; his heart beat slowly against her stomach. His eyelashes brushed her skin as he stroked her body lazily. Sam seemed content to linger in the scents and the warmth of their lovemaking, and she hugged the moment to her. Stroking his mussed hair, she realized how much she liked soothing Sam.

Raising up on his elbow, Sam caressed her cheek, running his hand downward to place his palm over her stomach. The gesture was strangely possessive and Dallas shifted beneath it uncomfortably. She waited for him to say something, anything devastating. Wasn't that what T.J. always did? she thought absently, running her fingers through Sam's crisp hair.

Dallas held still, wanting Sam to stay with her, yet fearing that now he had seen her inadequacies. Her cheeks burned as she remembered her shameless demands.

His finger circled the tip of her breast while he moved his thigh against hers slowly. When she looked at him, he grinned his most wicked, devastatingly sexy grin. He pulled out his dimples with all the effect of a sleepy, huggable, tamed wolf. The laugh lines deepened around his smoky eyes. "That was good for starters," he drawled in a low rich tone that started miniature tom-toms beating within her.

While Sam's big warm hand stroked her inner thighs, Dallas found herself returning his knowing, hungry grin. "Come here, sweet pea," he urged huskily after a soft, knowing chuckle. "Let me hear those hungry little purring sounds you make when we're—"

"Do not." She resisted acknowledging the prowling, stalking fingers and his rumbling, conspiratorial laughter.

"Okay. Then what about one delighted cry—muted of course—with trembling little purrs afterward? Or could you just sort of chant my name again like I've never heard it before?" he asked before his mouth hungrily sought hers.

Later she snuggled to him, savored the warmth and acknowledged with a blush that he had drawn every previously mentioned sound of delight from her.

She smiled, allowing her fingers to smooth the hair on his chest. She had caused some intriguing masculine sounds herself.

In the dawn, Sam stretched carefully, to avoid dislodging the softness wedged against his side. He breathed lightly, prolonging the moment when Dallas awoke. Catching the scent of her hair, Sam turned slightly to inhale the sweet-pea fragrance and savor the flow of her body down his.

Had he taken advantage of her rum-tinged weakness?

Sam scowled against the strand of red-brown hair clinging to his morning stubble. He'd never taken advantage of a woman before; he'd chosen ones who knew what to expect. But Dallas wasn't that type of woman. He'd known from the first that she was untutored and sweet.

Her body tightened, her breathing changed, and Sam waited.

When her eyes opened, Sam recognized the raw fear and pain scurrying around inside.

His anger surged to the surface before he could trim it.

"I want to know who did this to you," he demanded unevenly, fighting the urge to hold her down and make her answer his question. When Dallas's well-kissed mouth began to firm stubbornly, Sam knew that a field of cotton rosebuds wasn't the place to sort out his problems with the Pendragon virus.

He'd caught the puzzled frown before she'd turned away. The line of her back was tense and vulnerable. Dallas didn't want a repeat performance; he'd have to be granite not to recognize the symptoms.

"I can't have this happen again, Sam," she said quietly, and the sound of his emptiness went roaring through him.

He fought the urge to make her listen, to wrap her in his arms and coax her into loving him....

Sam's fist crumbled a spray of cotton rosebuds. Who the hell had ever loved him? "Have it your way," he said between his teeth, wanting to slip back into the soft, sweet night and her arms.

Then, because he was hurt and fighting mad, too, Sam did what he knew best—he lashed out at her. "Call me when you're in the mood again."

When her body tightened as though taking a blow, Sam felt his stomach contract painfully. She turned slowly, drawing the sheet between them. "Sam, I'm sorry."

"What the hell do you mean—sorry?" Sam wanted to tear away the past, lock onto the future and never let Dallas go!

"This is my fault. I take full responsibility and it won't happen again."

"You had a weak moment, right?" Sam demanded rawly, wondering if his heartbeat would ever return to normal.

"Something like that," she agreed, looking away into the rain dripping beyond the window.

Who was she remembering? Why should he care? He'd had her, hadn't he?

Why wasn't it enough? Why didn't he have enough pride to walk out now?

Why did he want to linger with Dallas as long as he could?

The afternoon before Christmas, Sam hid in his office. He'd avoided the secretaries who seemed to regard him in a new, endearing light. He'd sidestepped Debbie Wynbroski's attempt to snare him beneath the mistletoe ball in the employee lounge.

This morning, he'd been thinking about Dallas and had almost missed an important point in the company's new merger agreement. Sam ran his fingers through his longish hair. In three short weeks, he'd been totally absorbed by the Pendragon family. He knew exactly how Billy rubbed his eyes when he was tired; he knew exactly when Nikki decided to dig in her heels and argue.

He knew when Dallas needed a cup of tea. *And when she'd decided to back off from the relationship.* Sam wanted to free-fall into an affair, wrap himself in Dallas and her family. But Dallas skirted the issue and him with all the markings of one badly burned by an experience.

He smiled softly, remembering the way her eyes looked up at him after lovemaking. Soft and curious, wondering eyes.

Quite a feeling, he mused—Dallas's softness warming him beneath the quilt in the confines of the antique four-poster bed.

Quite a feeling knowing that memories of another man shared that bed with them. Sam found himself grinding his teeth each time he thought about Dallas's shy, tentative hands fluttering over him as though she expected—expected what?

In his lifetime, Sam had rolled with the blows and had landed a few himself. But the one thing he wasn't taking easily was that Dallas measured him against another man.

The thought hurt; it caught him in the belly with the force of a fighter's punch. For a man who'd never wanted lingering affairs, Sam found himself thinking of ways to snare Dallas.

In another week, he'd be expected to move. A cold shiver slid through him. He hadn't slept in his penthouse for weeks and dreaded the stylish, modular glass-and-steel building. It appealed to him as much as an iceberg cavern.

Running his hand through his hair again, Sam grimaced, staring into the gray cloud banks encompassing the bay. And Sam knew exactly how he would feel without the Pendragon family—exactly like Washington's Mount Rainier, alone and snow-capped in the distance.

Dallas's laughter echoed behind his office door, and Sam listened intently to the low musical sound. Sam turned, alert and tracking the sound carefully. He'd been keeping his distance, trying not to push a situation that he didn't understand himself. But there were just some things a man knew he had to do. And right now Dallas was near the Christmas mistletoe ball. For the present, problems with her past or not, Sam intended to use every mistletoe ball he could when Dallas's lips were in the vicinity....

Dallas turned, sensing someone at her back. Someone tall and warm and impatient placed a hand on her shoulder—a strong, possessive hand faintly scented like Nikki's doll. This morning, Sam had stuffed the children into Bertha's cab in a cloud of sweet-smelling powder.

She averted her head to shield her smile. Though she was badly frightened of being hurt again, her feminine senses started humming when Sam acted like a gentleman come calling. And for all Sam's defensive ways, he treated her in a very courtly manner. With a little pang of sadness, she thought about the life without Sam that waited for her.

Sam loomed over her, a strand of hair crossing his forehead. Behind his glasses, his eyes were intent as he watched her mouth. "You're standing beneath the mistletoe ball, sweet pea," he whispered before drawing her into his arms.

"Oooh," Emily cooed in the distance before Dallas found herself responding to Sam's sweet kiss. His lips rubbed against hers gently, his breath brushing her skin.

His heart beat steadily beneath her palm as he rubbed his cheek against hers. "Don't get any ideas, Ms. Pendragon. Just take it as a gesture of Christmas cheer," he said roughly, then his arms trembled around her, gathering her against him.

"Sweet," Emily commented as Dallas moved deeper into the kiss, dismissing the rest of the party. "Any other takers?"

"My turn," Debbie Wynbroski stated firmly, edging between them.

Dallas noted the way Sam's mouth clung to hers as though he resented being detached from her. Wild, primitive glee went skittering through her when he shot Emily a low-browed, menacing look, and his neck began to sink into his shoulders.

As the women began hooting and surged to surround Sam, his eyes widened. "Do something," he whispered hoarsely from the corner of his mouth, eyeing the approaching women warily.

"It's Christmas. And you started it," she returned, perching on a desk and crossing her arms. For the first time since Sam had been so furious with her, she began to feel lighthearted. He hadn't been totally unaffected by their night of lovemaking. Sam had a way of giving her self-esteem a big boost. "You didn't say please."

"Please?" Sam gritted through his teeth, glaring at her.

"Uh-uh. You're on your own."

Catching a glance of Sam's threatening expression, Dallas grinned cheerfully. "See yah," she murmured, stepping back to let Debbie get a better grip on Sam's muscular neck. "Line forms to the right," she called, stepping aside as the first wave of women passed her on their way to Sam.

"I'm calling the accounting, packaging and shipping departments." Emily punched the intercom button with a vengeance and smirked widely. "He's been due for this for a long time."

"How many women?" Dallas asked, her grin widening as two women pressed Sam between them. With a stiff grace Sam dutifully lowered his lips.

"Forty...and every one of them has been waiting for years. Edna Fairhair is saturating her lips with vitamin E right now. You know Edna—she was a wrestler before working in loading."

They watched a mother of seven grown children bend Sam backward and kiss him. "He's okay," Emily said absently. "He's just got this thing about centering in on business and forgetting everything else. He really had no idea of the stress problems or the ways to solve them. I think it hurt him to find out how thoughtless and too busy he'd been to realize.... You've been good for him."

Later, Dallas arrived home before Sam, carrying Emily's thoughts with her. She wanted Christmas Eve to be special for them all, a memory to last when he was striding through his domain in a replay of Attila the Hun. While she wasn't magnificent in some womanly areas, she could give him a slice of Christmas cheer to remember. She had enjoyed setting the scene—from bubbling potpourri to lasagna baking in the oven. Sam's favorite double-dutch chocolate cake was topped with richer frosting and studded with maraschino cherries.

Curling on the cabbage roses, dressed in a flowing dark blue caftan, Dallas sipped her oolong tea and reloaded the camera. She wanted to capture the expression on the children's face as they opened their gifts.

And she wanted a memory to savor when Sam left her alone.

Her thoughts danced like the flickering candlelight in the dark room.... She didn't love him. She couldn't. Sam— house husband, child-sitter—was a holiday mirage.

Sam had merely risen to a challenge presented to him. When the wager was completed, he'd slide back into his comfortable, untouched mode and his Lincoln without the slightest remorse. Dallas could feel the ache build painfully, the burning of tears behind her eyelids.

He'd been there when she needed him. He'd taken and he'd given. She missed his arms enfolding her against the cold night. Her old fashioned four-poster bed really needed Sam in it to complete the picture. All dark skin covered by just the right amount of hair, he matched the rosebuds and the ruffles so well.

Dallas wiped the back of her hand across her damp eyes and sniffed. *Sam Loring could just*—Bertha roared into the driveway and honked. Nikki and Billy were laughing wildly, and Sam's footsteps sounded on the porch. The door swung open to reveal Sam carrying a squirming, giggling child beneath each arm.

"Hey, lady. Have you lost two bear hunters?" he asked, the laughter in his face dying as he slowly absorbed the Christmas scene. "I'm home," he said softly, easing the children to their feet, the light warming in his eyes.

"When can we open our presents?" the children asked, tossing their coats aside to run to the tree.

"After supper, we're going to church. I baked a chocolate cake. Then you can open your presents," Dallas answered absently, concentrating on Sam's deliberate movements. He closed the door behind him with the air of a man shutting out the world and his problems. The genuine air of a man coming home.

He stripped off his coat and walked slowly toward her. "Hi," he said as though she were his alone, tossing the coat onto a chair.

"Hi, yourself," she returned, thinking that with his hair ruffled by the wind and his dark cheeks cold and ruddy, Sam Loring was absolutely, incredibly all hers.

Hers? She echoed the thought, turning it over.

He needed her.

Oh, no, he didn't. Sam needed business and women without children who knew when to stop loving. He didn't need a clinging vine.

Oh, no, she couldn't love him. Oh, no....

While the children inspected the packages for new ones, Sam knelt by her, taking her hand in his cold ones. "I'm suffering from lip burn and it's your fault," he complained softly, watching her mouth. Raising her hand to his lips, he nuzzled the warmth.

He was teasing and when he grinned, pulling out the thousand-watt dimples, Dallas couldn't resist returning the favor. "Hard day at the office, dear?" she asked, fighting a smile. Sam might prefer another sort of woman, but she really liked petting his battered-tom-cat image.

Sam looked at her as if he needed her touch, her kisses or just her spare time. He looked like Baghdad coming back after straying into the cold, uncaring alley.

"When can I have my present?" he returned silkily, rubbing her hand against his cheek. "Like a kiss when the office staff and the kids aren't watching. I think you owe me."

Could they be friends? she wondered briefly as she remembered the mistletoe mob at the office. Sam had taken the maneuver in stride and gallantly allowed the stiff image of a company boss to slip, endearing him to his staff. She patted his jaw sympathetically. "I've made it up to you with lasagna and cake."

Nibbling at her fingertips, Sam grinned. "Mmm. Real food. All this—" his gaze slid down the blue caftan, lingering on the curve of soft thigh exposed by the slit "—and she can cook, too." He raised an eyebrow and leered wickedly at her. "What I had in mind wasn't food and you know it."

"Really?" Dabbling in Sam's tastes could become addictive, she decided as she fluttered her lashes at him.

Billy crawled into Sam's lap and hugged him. "Sam and me got a secret, don't we, Sam?"

Nikki squealed and jumped on Sam's back. "Me and Mommy got a secret, too... and you don't know what it is, Billy. "Cause you're a little kid and you'd tell."

"Would not."

"Would, too."

Later, Sam sat beside Dallas in church, watching the children sing in the children's choir. With his arm resting behind her on the pew, Sam looked like any other proud father. When he smiled down at her, she felt a warm glow settle within her. They were a family, together at Christmas, caring for each other and rejoicing in the baby's birth that changed the world.

When they opened presents at the house, Sam folded Dallas's hand within his. Nikki's new baby doll fit perfectly into Sam's crib; the girl's eyes lighted each time she looked his way. Not as subtle, Billy ran into his room and began lugging out "stuff" to fill his special box.

Sam handled the children's gift of after-shave carefully, placing it on the table as he stood. "I'll be right back."

Sitting on the floor with the children, Dallas rocked the crib with her toe and helped Billy choose only the best "special stuff" for his box.

"Dallas," Sam said quietly behind her.

When she turned, he placed a walnut quilt rack rubbed to a rich sheen in front of her. Folded neatly across it was a patchwork quilt. The design of delicate stitching swirled across pieces of worn flannel, faded cotton gingham. Kneeling beside it, Dallas carefully ran her fingers across the walnut and the quilt. On the underside, a faded rose flannel had been pieced together. "Oh, Sam," she whispered, feeling her throat tighten with emotion. "This is lovely."

"It's yours," he said, lowering his neck slightly. He looked away and swallowed as though embarrassed. "The quilt, too."

Running her hand across the wood, Dallas felt her heart shift and warm. "Sam, did you make this just for me?"

He shifted restlessly, his neck sinking into his shoulders in the familiar gesture. "Of course," he said roughly. Behind the glasses, his smoky eyes darkened. "Do you like it or not?"

Rising to her feet, Dallas couldn't resist standing on tiptoe and kissing Sam's overworked lips. He'd given her a part of himself, a gift that she could cherish alone in the fields of lonely cotton rosebuds. "It's beautiful. Thank you."

"You're welcome," he returned stiffly as a dark flush crept up from his throat. For a hard-nosed businessman, Sam looked definitely embarrassed. The moment was one to be treasured.

Running her hand across the well-washed quilt, Dallas teased, "And you can quilt, too."

He shrugged lightly, widening his legs in a defensive stance. "Someone special made it. It suits you."

"Someone very special?" A little hurt twanged inside Dallas. She couldn't rest beneath a quilt created by his past lover—

"Granny Dunnaway." Sam looked away. "A hill woman who smoked a corncob pipe and blistered my backside more times than I want to remember. After my...mother ran off, Granny bribed the juvenile officer with a jug of moonshine when he came for me...made me hide in the outhouse.... She'd want you to have it."

Dallas fought the tears blurring her eyes. "Oh, Sam."

"Oh, sweet pea," he teased softly. "Granny was tough as leather. I cut and stacked three cords of wood when we didn't need any. Then she made me this quilt. She'd want you to have it."

Sam had revealed very little of his past, and Dallas hugged the insight to her, his special gift.

While the children played, unaware of the two adults locking gazes, Dallas whispered, "I've got your present tucked away."

"I can't wait," he murmured huskily, placing his hand on the back of her neck to draw her closer.

"Uh-uh." She fought the urge to cling to him. "I'll be right back. Come on, kids. Let's get Sam's present."

Minutes later, Nikki and Billy presented Sam with a huge box, gaily decorated with a red bow. "From us," Billy announced proudly.

"It's silly," Nikki said haughtily, cradling her new baby doll.

"Is not!" Billy stated with decided male arrogance. "Girls' stuff is silly."

"Open it, Sam," Dallas urged gently as Sam's large hands trembled on the box.

For a man who had made a corporation his life, Sam appeared filled with emotion. "You didn't have to—"

Because he seemed so vulnerable, needing her, Dallas sat on the arm of the couch and placed her hand on his shoulder. She rubbed the tense muscles gently. "Get with it, Loring," she urged lightly in his ear.

Sam began unwrapping carefully, his hands shaking as he discovered the engine of a toy train. The muscles and cords of his throat tightened beneath her light touch. And because Sam needed petting, Dallas smoothed his hair, feeling the crisp texture cling to her skin the way Sam was to her life.

"It's something to show you how much we appreciate you helping with the grizzly bears and the housework."

"I'm a rotten cook," he admitted quietly, running his fingertips across the new shiny red caboose. "Those were really microwave potatoes the other night. I burned the real ones. There's more to this home-and-family bit than meets the eye."

The unsteady timbre of his voice caused her to ache. Big, tough Sam Loring was honestly touched by the gift. He eased the sections of track from the box, placing them carefully on the floor.

"Do you like it, Sam?" Billy asked, sinking to the floor to place the toy caboose on the track. "Isn't it the best ever?"

"The best ever," Sam echoed, his broad shoulders shuddering just once.

Dallas spotted a suspicious moisture behind Sam's lenses, and smiled knowingly. Tough guy Sam Loring was having an encounter of the emotional kind. "Get to it, Loring," she ordered, touching his arm. "You know you want to."

"I suppose you think this lets you off the hook," he said seductively, sliding to the floor with Billy. "But to keep the record straight, it doesn't...."

He nodded, sliding a hand around her calf and caressing it gently. "Nice try, though," he said, unpacking the rest of the train set and fitting it together. "I've always wanted one...."

The tiny train chugged through tunnels and switched rails while Billy and Sam lay on their stomachs engineering the feats. "Silly stuff," Nikki said with a delicate sneer, tucking her doll blanket inside the crib. "Boys."

Later, Dallas drifted off to sleep as the little train whoo-whooed merrily around the track. She awoke to Sam wrapping her in the quilt and holding her on his lap.

"Whatcha doin', Mr. Sam?" she asked sleepily, comforted by the warmth and strength of his touch on a cold Christmas night.

"Holding my best girl." Sam kissed her forehead and tucked her against him. "Go back to sleep. I just want to hold you. Thanks for the train, Dallas. And the visit to church. I haven't felt so... well, it was nice."

Because Sam needed her, Dallas wrapped her arm around his neck and toyed with the hair brushing his collar. "I'll cut your hair tomorrow when I do Billy's," she murmured sleepily.

Tensing slightly, Sam shrugged. "A barber can do it."

"Don't be afraid. I won't mark you for life." She sighed against his warm throat as she drifted off to sleep.

"Maybe I already am.... I don't think a flu shot is going to take care of this virus," he whispered unsteadily, holding her tighter.

Nine

"Hold still," Dallas ordered, tilting Sam's head to one side while she combed and snipped his hair.

While the children played with the toys placed in their Christmas stockings by Santa Claus, Sam savored every touch of Dallas's cinnamon-roll scented hands. He'd never spent a time like this one, lolling in the warmth of a family filled with Christmas spirit.

Dallas wore a curious but satisfied look. Like a woman who needed to care for others—her children and himself, of course. Beneath the smugness there was also a fear that Sam knew only time could soften.

Stretching comfortably beneath her touch, Sam allowed his eyes to close. Dallas needed his protection. She needed him.

Quite a feeling, he thought with pleasure—knowing that someone needed him. A warm, fuzzy feeling that filled all the rough edges of his life. He allowed himself a small smile. Dallas didn't know exactly how much she needed him in all areas of her life, including the sensual one. She'd been shocked by herself, embarrassed by her needs. Despite the control she managed now, Dallas had once forgotten herself. With him. It was just a matter of time before he had her seeing things his way.

Thoroughly enjoying her care, Sam felt like a cat sunning on a warm window sill. With a bowl of milk waiting for him. Drifting along dreamily under Dallas's intent care, Sam wondered absently if next Christmas he could replace her plastic manger scene with a hand-carved one.

Dallas tilted his head, angling it for a better cut. She frowned, studying her handiwork. "I know you're running short on money Sam," she murmured absently, brushing a snipped hair from his chin. "I can loan you enough to get you through until the first of the month. Or I'll get the grocery bill this week and you can repay me."

"No," he said flatly, catching her wrist and jumping off his imaginary warm window sill. Dallas needed to know a few of his personal rules. "I've never had a woman support me yet."

A quick shaft of pain crossed Dallas's expression before she eased her wrist away and returned to snipping his hair. "I was offering a loan, not support, Sam."

The thoughts of discussing his deflated wallet with a woman who had stormed his body molecules like a virus caused Sam to straighten. Santa had stuffed Sam's stocking with toothpaste, razors and new black dress socks, and now the woman he most wanted to take care of was asking if he needed support. In Sam's book of rules, he did all the running.

He frowned, replaying his last thoughts. Up to now, he'd always called the shots in his relationships, never letting anyone share his problems. Letting Dallas inside him wasn't easy. Neither was admitting that he was wrong about the difficulties of a woman's working world.

Not wanting to spoil a memory he'd need to warm him later, Sam shifted uneasily as her fingers swept down the back of his neck. "So maybe I jumped the gun. I'm not used to someone else picking up my tabs," he managed stiffly.

"Our tabs, Sam," she corrected, her green eyes lighting with humor. "You know, sooner or later, you're going to have to admit that running a home with children and working isn't easy."

Running a soothing finger along his eyebrows, Dallas grinned. "Admit it. I won . . . say it out loud. I dare you."

When Dallas touched him, Sam had the feeling of being petted. *He liked Dallas petting him.* He also had the feeling she could wrap him around her cinnamon-scented finger. The thought startled him. Pre-Dallas, no one teased or messed with him. If he were that cat on the windowsill, he'd probably roll over to have his belly scratched. The thought of Dallas touching his stomach started Sam wondering when he'd have her alone again. "Don't rub it in . . . I'll give you a maybe."

When her grin widened, Sam suddenly became lightheaded. "Okay, you won. I've glanced over some of your proposals and they don't seem too far out of line. We'll start working on them in the new year."

Dallas's low, delighted giggle made Sam's whole body feel light and airy. "Okay, Pendragon. Cut the gloating and finish the job," he said, returning her infectious grin.

The day after Christmas, Sam returned to work, leaving Dallas sleeping in a bed where he very much wanted to join her. Revving up Bertha, he pulled out of the driveway with a feeling of leaving a life he desperately wanted and needed.

Traditionally Sam used the after-Christmas lull to work without the interference of calls and appointments. This year, the quiet had lost its appeal. Manned by a skeleton staff for the holidays, the office seemed cold and drained of cheer. Emily was visiting her grandchildren, leaving Sam to the mercy of a replacement who needed a dictaphone.

By noon, Sam gave up working and sank into his thoughts as he watched the few people on the sidewalk below. Most of them had parcels in hand, and Sam guessed absently that they were returning gifts.

Sam switched to watching the expensive paneling on his walls. *He* felt like a returned gift, one taken out of the shop on approval that now had to be restored to the shelf. Every impulse within him said to go home and play with Billy and his toy train.

Every nerve ending said to go home to Dallas and listen for the low melodic sound of her laughter.

Was she wearing that African caftan, the one with the thigh-high slit and the embroidered neckline that shifted when she bent?

Pouring Dallas's hot vegetable soup from his thermos into a bowl, Sam wondered who would chase household bears? Who would powder Nikki's doll's rubber backside when he left? "Not that damn Beau," Sam growled, spooning out the lima beans Dallas had generously dumped into the soup.

What about Dallas's trim backside? Who would be touching it?

Who would warm his lap next Christmas Eve and snuggle against him as though he were all that mattered.

Sam had never been nestled in the warmth of a home, children and a woman who looked at him with sleepy, sexy witch's eyes. Now that he had experienced all that, Sam wanted the whole picture.

The new year without the Pendragon family loomed like a cold, dark abyss before Sam. He spooned another lima bean into his trash can and began reading Dallas's proposals intently.

Taking second place to his efforts at money-stretching casseroles and managing a family, the reports had never had his full attention. They were detailed, projected and outlined in the professional manner that Sam had expected. Sam frowned and nudged The Whammy Plan aside; he didn't like that one at all. He couldn't see himself shifting into Emily's practical chair. But the other proposals were fleshed out with backup material and costs, and could be braided into Brice's employee plan. "They're too good," Sam muttered darkly, turning to his other paperwork.

"They need a few kinks to keep the cogs from turning too fast."

Sam flipped through her summary presentation and tossed it aside. The Pendragon virus had invaded his life and altered his focus on what he wanted, how he wanted to live. Dallas had unknowingly intruded into his comfortable no-strings life-style; she had filtered through his protective shell. It was too late for immunization in Delilah's bed.

Driving home that night, Sam had the sinking feeling that the house would have disappeared. But it stood against the cold drizzle, the lights in the windows. He entered the front door to inhale the scents of pot roast, apple pie and home. Dallas turned from the stove, her eyes lighting as she smiled at him. Billy called loudly, "Sam's home." And suddenly Sam felt fear clawing wildly at him. A few more days and he'd be back in the cold.

And Beau would hover like a vulture, waiting to kiss Dallas on her doorstep.

"The hell he will," Sam stated with all the possession he felt, closing out the cold beyond the small house as he picked up Billy and hefted him into the air playfully.

Over the next five days, Sam shielded his pride and his heart. He dreamed about Dallas walking toward him with her arms open. Like a miser hoarding gold, he absorbed every tiny scent and sound, the colors and texture of Dallas.

Did she ache as he did? he wondered as he'd caught her lingering gaze with his own.

Would she miss him? he wondered as she'd slid her gaze from his.

Was it reality or his dreams when her hand had brushed his and trembled? Dallas's voice had lowered and softened during the last few days of his visit, and Sam fantasized wildly that she would ask him to stay.

On the thirty-first of December, Sam moved out with promises that he would keep: He'd call and see the children often. When he glanced at Dallas as he stood in the doorway with his suitcase, she shifted and looked away. She'd be glad to not have him underfoot, he thought moodily as Nikki wrapped her arms around him. And Sam wished Dallas was waiting in line.

She wasn't. Her hands gripped the wood railing as firmly as Sam had grasped his pre-Pendragon virus life. When their eyes met, Sam drew his mouth into a smile. Unable to say anything to her, he turned away with the grim knowledge that he was leaving a big slice of himself smeared on her front steps.

He hunched his shoulders and drew up his denim jacket against the cold drizzle and the aching emptiness within him.

That night, New Year's Eve, Sam propped his worn boots on his penthouse desk. He ignored the oil Bertha had spit on his jeans and squinted at the remaining half bottle of whiskey—which he intended to drink.

On a side table, the toy train chugged merrily through tunnels and over hills, guided by Sam's switchbox controls.

The train passed two doll children and Sam grimaced. He already missed caring for Nikki's doll while he studied a cookbook.

He'd planned to sink into the paperwork crushed beneath his boots. But remembering Dallas's soft fingers as she cut his hair had sent him over the edge.

Closing his eyelids, Sam recalled Dallas's intent expression . . . the tilt of her head as she'd studied her handiwork. He'd never been made over in his life. Never really had a woman touch him with lingering hands as though he were her special project. As though he needed petting. Surrounded by her touch and scents, Sam had been afraid to move and had longed for the moment to stretch into eternity.

The warm little house, filled with kids and love and Dallas nestled cozily apart from his world. . . . Nothing lasts forever. The mirage was over.

He'd experienced a big concentrated chunk of the things that he'd never wanted before—family, love and a woman who knew how to make him feel needed and warm inside.

Wrapped in his glass-and-chrome tomb, without the potpourri scents and the children, he felt like hell. In the old days, when he'd needed to strike out at the world, he'd find some nice accommodating construction worker. One the size of a freighter and mean clear through. Slugging it out with Dallas wasn't possible.

"That's the problem with viruses. They invade your immune system. Once you're infected, you can't fight 'em."

In an effort to self-inoculate, Sam sipped from the bottle, the whiskey burning his throat. In the week after Christmas, Dallas had worked harder, the circles darkening beneath her haunted eyes. She didn't need him messing in her life, messing it up. Rosebuds and backwoods leather didn't mix. He'd slipped into her soft little loving world for a month, had let the warmth trickle around him, and had known that he'd have to leave before he hurt her.

"Hell, what do I know about keeping her safe?" he muttered, tilting the bottle to his lips.

Dallas wouldn't know about keeping the score even, about clean endings. About saying meaningless things like, "I'll call," or "See you soon."

She'd seen him with his business-suit veneer.

He'd seen her lounging in the cotton rosebuds and nothing else—

Sam groaned, needing the warmth of Dallas's soft body snuggling against him.

Dallas was as afraid of a commitment as he. Sam digested the thought with another burning sip.

He didn't want to hurt her. And he didn't need any more scars.

Hell, he didn't know the simplest thing about loving. *It wouldn't work.*

Why not?

Because he was afraid. Somewhere along the way, he'd shucked a piece of himself. Paid his dues and came out too tough for a tenderhearted woman like Dallas. Some jerk had cut her heart, and she didn't need to be hurt again.

Feeling thoroughly cold, Sam sat and stared at the little train.

At midnight, Dallas sucked the juice from a chocolate-covered cherry candy and wiped away her tears. "What's New Year's Eve for if not to cry?" she asked the feather bird nestled in the candle ring.

Nestling deeper in her four-poster bed, she tugged Sam's quilt closely around her. The crumpled empty wrappers rustled as she reached for a new box of candy.

Watching the candle flicker within its holly-and-pinecone wreath, Dallas thought of Sam. He'd be happy now, returning to his penthouse and his smooth, expensive lifestyle. Ripping away the box's cellophane wrapper, she ignored the fresh tears creeping down her cheeks.

She sniffed, sucking more cherry-flavored juice.

She should have never allowed herself to be drawn in by a Southern drawl and dimples. At thirty-nine, just when things were rolling along safely in her life, Sam had come along. She'd fallen for his dimples, Southern drawl and battered tomcat image.

Then he'd packed Bertha and ran for freedom, just like T.J. Except Sam had a haunted, sheepdog look about him when he walked down the steps.

"Well, more like a tomcat kicked out in the rain," she mused to the feather bird.

She shrugged, dislodging Granny's quilt, which she pulled tightly back around her. Fighting bears by herself wasn't the fun it used to be. Exploring a lump in the quilt's folds, she extracted Sam's black dress socks mottled with bleach spots. Wiping away the tears, Dallas stuck her hand in it and wriggled her fingers through the hole at the toe.

Sam Loring would admit that the working woman's world wasn't a bowl of chocolate-covered cherries.

Her proposals were perfected, including The Whammy Plan for Executives.

She'd succeeded—but she'd lost Sam. She liked caring for him. Loved the unexpected pleasure softening his hard face as the train went whizzing by him.

If he were in her four-poster bed now, she doubted that she could restrain herself. Dallas groaned again just as the phone near her bed rang. "Hello."

Nettled by the silence at the other end, Dallas sniffed. "Look you, if this is a crank call—same to you, buddy."

"Are you crying?" Sam's slurred Southern voice asked.

Dallas's fingers stopped wriggling in the sock hole. A person couldn't even get a really good cry going without interruption. Just when she wanted to wallow in chocolates and misery, Sam would choose to call. "Have a cold. Why are you calling?"

"I would like to know just what you're wearing, please," he stated in a too-proper, distinct tone.

Not wanting to give him an edge on her dismals, Dallas returned, "I'll tell you if you tell me."

Sam breathed heavily once, as though preparing for a difficult survey. Then after a long silence, he stated proudly, "Boots."

"A nightgown."

"The flannel one with rosebuds?" Sam asked in his bear growl while his train choo-chooed in the background.

"Uh-huh."

"Oh, God, I thought so," he groaned before the line went dead. Dallas hung up, feeling colder and older than ever.

When the phone rang again, Dallas jerked the receiver to her ear. Sam had disturbed her entire life, the least he could do was to let her suck chocolate-center juice in peace. "Lay off, Loring. You lost and you know it. I couldn't care less if you're wearing nothing but boots and a smile. You keep your side of the deal, and I'll keep mine. You've been listening with an open mind, and I appreciate that, no matter if the project is approved by the board or not. But I don't apreciate you trying to remind me that we . . . we—"

"Honey?" Lisa's soft voice crooned above an off-key rendition of *Auld Lang Syne*. "I just wanted to wish you a Happy New Year."

"Oh, Mother!" Was it the hour or the brink of a new year that caused her to say just what she meant to the wrong person?

Glasses clinked near Lisa. "Edward and I are at a party. I can hear those chocolate wrappers rustle. Are you having a bad night? And what's more important, is Sam really wearing nothing but boots? Why aren't you all together? Or in the altogether, together?"

"He packed his toy train and ran at the first chance," Dallas stated sulkily.

"Don't ever compare a man like Sam to the likes of T.J., Dallas, dear," Lisa warned softly. "Did you ever buy that peignoir set? Did you ever give Sam any indication that you wanted to play in his sandbox with his toys?"

"Mother—" She'd played with Sam, and now could she forget? Every time the Deons started nuzzling, Dallas shivered with cold . . . Sam's arms were so warm—

Lisa laughed softly. "He's gotten to you, hasn't he? He's just a little sweet boy beneath all those lovely muscles. Have a Happy New Year, dear. I'll call soon."

On January 2, Sam lounged behind his desk like a lion waiting for a lamb chop while Dallas spread her proposal before him. He'd returned to his gray suit and businessman's shell.

While Dallas explained the innovative child-care center idea, complete with remodeling costs, Sam tapped his pencil. "That's a big chunk of budget dollars," he said curtly when she finished.

"Think of it as an investment to cut employee absenteeism."

"You don't think the mothers will be distracted by having their children nearby?"

Dallas looked away from Sam's penetrating gray eyes, which were flicking curious glances at her as though trying to see into her. If he were able to scan her emotions, he'd get a pretty icy picture. Or maybe red-hot flames. Maybe he could pack all those December memories in a box and forget them, but she couldn't. Where did he get off, anyway?

They'd made love, hadn't they?

What was she, a pre-Christmas aperitif? Why hadn't he called again? "Less distracted than if they were worrying about their children getting good care. With a company nurse and skilled babysitters at hand, the children would get the attention they needed. Remember how you felt when Billy and Nikki were sick?"

"How are the kids?" he asked absently, scanning the stack of reports she had removed from her briefcase. He flipped through the graphs and figures she had prepared for the job-sharing proposal. "Did Nikki get over her upset stomach?"

"They're fine." *How are you?* Dallas longed to ask as she scanned the lean cheeks hiding Sam's dimples. His neatly clipped hair caught the winter light passing through the windows, now gray appearing in the black strands. "How's Bertha?" Sam looked up at her, his smoky eyes cool behind the lenses.

"Fine," he returned in that gravelly steel voice that had lost its beguiling Southern magnolia tones. "A little first-gear problem."

He's run for cover, she thought, arranging her cost-summation sheet before him. *What man wouldn't after experiencing her lack of control?*

Sam glanced at his watch. "Let's see the rest of your presentation. I've got another appointment."

Just like that: The chocolate cake was nice. Thank you for the truth. And the romp. Who needed an inflexible tyrant with a broken nose? "I can see you're very receptive to change, Mr. Loring," Dallas snapped scathingly. "If you're going to back out, I'll expect repayment for costs."

Logic told her that she wanted no part of a relationship with Sam; her heart and body were angry because he'd obviously forgotten a moment that she'd remember her entire life.

"Change isn't the problem. I admit that a working mother has a difficult time in the workplace. You've seen that I've experienced it firsthand. But Brice doesn't throw time and money around easily. I'll work with you on these programs myself, and we'll move into them slowly. I can see the business day as an easy first step. But the rest of the programs will have to be integrated into policy. It could take months, but I'm open to your suggestions now. We can start work . . . tonight at my place."

She didn't want to be anywhere in his vicinity. Right now, her fingertips ached to trace the deep line running between his eyebrows. To smooth that rebellious gray hair in his left eyebrow. Offices were fine . . . well, other than that one incident behind his desk. But a penthouse was an intimate setting. "I get the idea. A conditional trade-off."

"I'd be a fool to go half-cocked into anything this big." Sam's voice had lowered, edged in raw steel as he leaned down toward her. "You know that up front. We'll work together on this thing, smoothing out the rough edges."

He shrugged, tightening his mouth grimly. "You may have to swallow the fact that you'll have to work with me closely in the next few months. But you'll find that we can do a better job together."

Sam was the one man she didn't want near her, especially for "the next few months." Beau, by comparison, wouldn't start her nerves clipping along at too fast a pace.

"No one asked you to do anything but have an open mind," Dallas said crisply, stacking her proposals neatly into her briefcase. "I suppose you're going to take your sweet time about it, too."

"Stop bristling, Pendragon. I just don't want you to fall on that beautiful rear—"

"It's my rear, isn't it?" she began hotly. "So gallant. So trustworthy. You're—"

"I'm backing you, Dallas," Sam said slowly, watching her with narrowed eyes. "But don't get the idea that I'm putting my company at your fingertips. We have to move through the processes, blend carefully so that production and business aren't affected. Roughly, give the plans six months or so... a month for a proposal."

Sam thought her rear was beautiful. For a moment, Dallas just stared at him, digesting the thought. It was nonsense, she decided. If Sam wanted a woman, she'd know it. Like that night, she'd known well enough that Sam wanted her. Why didn't he now? Maybe T.J. was right.... "Working with you isn't easy," she said carefully. "I'd prefer an office environment."

Sam grinned slowly, wickedly. "Chicken."

"I'm very busy. We've just signed new contracts for stress schools and I'll have to train another aid." Dallas fussed with her proposals, feeling her body temperature rise as Sam leaned closer.

"For someone who goes around throwing challenges at nice men minding their own business, you're a chicken," he murmured against her neck, and Dallas jumped with the impulses rioting through her. She wanted to wrap her arms around him and—

Dallas took a deep breath. She was a professional. She could handle Sam Loring. On any terms. "Okay, what's first?" she asked, dismissing Sam's dimpled smirk.

Moving behind his desk, Sam sat down. "A meeting with the board. They've got to see this project as valuable in long-run terms, not as an expense that could be avoided. We'd better show results with the first project, and I'm recommending the job-sharing idea. You're going to have to work with the managers and the employees, Dallas. And keep me briefed. No notes, but daily conferences."

He tapped a pen on his desk. "I'm calling the shots from now on, Dallas. Telling me to shoo won't cut it. Since you're not comfortable with my place, we'll have to make do with the office and your place...that will work in neatly with my plans to visit Nikki and Billy." He smiled then, a slow full-of-confidence smile. "See? I'm ready to modify. I'm going into this thing with an open mind. See that you do the same."

Fighting the small flutter in her stomach, she returned Sam's predatory smile. He was up to no good!

Ten

"Shoo!" Sam threw a left smash into the punching bag, dancing around it. "She thinks she can shoo me away, does she? I'm taking the gloves off this time," he muttered, matching his one-two jabs with the words. "No more Mr. Nice Guy."

By the end of January, Sam's taut nerves and body needed the intense workout. He could see now that he'd blundered where nice guys didn't. He'd forced a situation before its time and now he'd just have to wade through the basics he had skipped. Dallas wasn't the kind to step out on a ledge easily and for a momentary thrill. The thought that she was alone in her rosebuds had caused Sam sleeplessness and a rough edge that Emily tagged as "...Sheer low-down orneriness. And you were coming along so nicely, too."

"Nice!" He threw a left upper cut into the bag, feeling stretched to his limits. For the first time in his life, Sam knew that one wrong move or word would cost him a future with Dallas.

He needed her in his life. So Sam had done what he knew best: he'd sketched out a ruthless plan to capture and isolate the Pendragon virus. He didn't want it spreading to other men, acquiring them along the way.

Sam jabbed at the punching bag, circling it with an intensity he intended to use on Dallas.

Sam zapped the bag with a right cross. He'd taken down some major heavyweights in his time by seeking out their weakness and then zooming in on them.

To start his strategy off right, Sam had sent her a large box of bonbons topped by a huge red bow. According to Lisa, Dallas ate chocolate-covered cherries when she was nervous. He instructed the candy maker to keep sending the boxes. In his brand of honor, you let the opponent see you coming.

When Dallas woke up in the morning, Sam had had breakfast waiting. He'd touched base with her several times during the day. Taking Emily's suggestion, he'd occasionally popped into the Pendragon offices with a basket lunch. He'd fought household bears at bedtime, and then had waited for when Dallas had her ritual cup of tea.

He liked her cabbage-rose couch. It was just small enough to place his arm on the back. From there he could stroke Dallas's smooth cheek. Or rub the taut muscles at the back of her neck.

Dallas was too tight, too nervous. "Scared stiff is more like it. She's not the only one."

Emily opened his gym door and grinned toothily. "Nikki Pendragon on line two."

Sam pivoted to her instantly. "What's wrong?"

Her grin widened. "It sounds serious." But Sam had already brushed past her on his way back to the office.

Had something happened to Dallas? Did Billy fall down stairs or play with tools that should be locked away? Forcing his fears aside, Sam said gently, "Hi, Nikki?"

One small sniff echoed loudly through his heart, stopping the quickening beat. By the second sniff, Sam found his hand strangling the receiver, his knuckles showing white beneath the skin. "Nikki, is something wrong?" he forced himself to ask calmly.

"The Sunbirds are all bringing their dads to a special meeting. We're supposed to fix box lunches and put on plays and sing and...oh, Mr. Sam, Mom said not to bother you." Nikki's rapid burst was followed by another heart-chilling sniff.

Dallas didn't want him—Sam swallowed, his throat too tight to accept the moisture. He didn't intend to be squeezed out of the Pendragon household, no matter what Dallas's fears were. The children needed him, and if Dallas would stop fighting him long enough— "I'd love to come, Nikki. I haven't had a good box lunch in my entire life. It's a date."

"But Mom said...." Nikki protested in a tone that sounded like she'd just gotten another Christmas present.

The thought that Dallas wanted to cancel his adoption papers drew Sam's neck down protectively. He could feel himself gearing up for a fight. The odd thing about it was, he really liked fighting with Dallas as much as he liked talking over a proposal. Or loving her into the rainy night.... He'd never been friends with a woman before, and without the white-hot sensual tension running between them, Dallas just could be his first female friend. "I'll call your mother and ask for permission to date my favorite girl. How about that, Nikki?"

"Great!" After excitedly relaying the details of the gala, Nikki's voice lowered. "Baghdad hasn't come home for a long time...Daddy. Mom says old toms sometimes just find another home. I like Baghdad, and Billy's just a kid—he cries sometimes. Do you think he'll come home?"

Old toms sometimes just find another home. Sam's mouth firmed as he reassured Nikki about the cat's return and offered to join the search party.

Hell, he'd found what he'd been looking for in one short month—Dallas's soft, caring touch. "This old tom isn't going anywhere," Sam muttered after saying goodbye.

He punched out the telephone number of Dallas's office. "What's this about not bothering me, Dallas?" he asked when she picked up the line.

"Stop snarling, Sam. I don't need the stress today," she warned lightly, but he ignored the tone.

"Stress, hell! You're creating stress. If Nikki wants to ask me to the Sunbirds box lunch, she can—"

"Sam." He knew she was fighting for control and didn't feel like giving her the edge. In his experience, once the pressure was on, it was best to keep it going.

Sam found himself grinning. Dallas shielded her base emotions from everyone else. But not from him. He'd felt her fire once, had found her fears, and he intended to make her recognize what she needed—him. "You need me, Dallas. Admit it. Nikki and Billy do, too. By the way, you viruses are all alike. You interfere with a perfectly good working system, mess around with the basics, then scoot on out without looking back—"

"What are you talking about?" Dallas's low husky voice had just the fighting edge to it that Sam wanted. The really nice thing about Dallas was that he could level with her.

Zeroing in on that tone, Sam felt himself smirking. He'd caught a cluster of secretaries talking about what excited them, and a favorite line in a movie yielded results that spanned from weak knees to hearts stopping. Deciding to give sweet-talking a try, Sam said, "I'm talking about soft sighs on my skin, sweet shy kisses, rain on the windows and rosebuds on the sheets, a demanding, sexy, witch-eyed woman with hair like liquid, silky copper and a body like I've never touched before. Of long, fascinating, silky legs that reach way up. Of low sultry whispers sweeping over me like intoxicating red wine. Of lips like fresh strawberries and arms that make me feel all new. I'm talking about sweet peas growing at the back door on an Appalachia moonlit night, of magnolias and fresh-baked bagels. Of commitments to last forever and of sharing mistletoe balls every year and watching Nikki and Billy grow up together and holding their children on our laps and of loving every single day of our lives together. I'm talking about you and me, caring for each other, needing and wanting and having it all between us.... And none of that has anything to do with T.J. McCall, Nikki and Billy or our contract. Think about it," he added lightly, cheerfully, and then he gently replaced the phone in the cradle.

Sam looked at the spot behind his desk where Dallas had first found her immunity-to-love slipping, and found himself grinning widely. "Let her chew on that," he said proudly before whistling a sexy *Blue Tango*. Dancing with an imaginary woman, Sam tangoed around his desk, bent his ladylove over his arm and kissed her soundly.

Arriving on Dallas's doorstep that night, Sam rubbed Baghdad's scarred ears with just the right roughness the cat preferred. Finding the tom wasn't difficult after he offered every child in the neighborhood a new bicycle. When in doubt, Sam followed his old rules: you have to put out to get what you want. And he wanted Dallas.

"Do your stuff, boy," he coached the purring tom as he waited for Dallas to answer the doorbell. "Slide right in there."

When Dallas opened the door, wearing her long electric-blue caftan, Sam found himself staring hungrily at her. "We're here." He managed to say before the children swooped down on the thin and grinning tomcat.

But Dallas crossed her arms across her breasts—which Sam had found himself remembering very well—and frowned up at him with all the warmth of a refrigerator. "Aren't you glad to see Baghdad?" Sam asked lightly, stepping past her and taking off his coat to hug the jubilant children.

"Of course, I'm glad to see the cat. What do you mean," she said between her teeth when he straightened to grin at her, "saying things like you did today?"

"Hmm?" Sam asked absently, settling himself on the floor to play with Billy's new dump truck. Edgy and miffed, Dallas's steamed look reminded Sam of the way she made love. Baghdad—acting his in-cahoots part—rubbed against Sam like an old, beloved friend. He purred so loudly, Dallas couldn't possibly ignore his happiness.

"I'll talk to you about the matter some other time," Dallas stated in her strictly-business-but-uncertain-about-herself tone.

Sam allowed his gaze to slowly wander up Dallas's long leg, exposed by the thigh-high slit. Wrapping his hand around her ankle, he caressed her skin with his thumb. "Let's start dating, sweet pea," he offered in a tone of honorable innocence. "Bowling, movies. With or without the children. Of course, I don't think they'll want to go to those dull plays that you enjoy so much. But I will. I'll try my best to understand the underlying, obscure meaning. I'll even let you drive Bertha to the junkyard. She's due for a new doorknob. We can scout out the wrecks together, okay?"

"Sounds like great fun," she said under her breath and in a sarcastic tone.

"Getting to you, aren't I?" he asked, scratching Baghdad's scarred ears roughly. When Dallas's cheeks began to flush, Sam lifted his eyebrows several times, teasing her with his imitation of Tom Selleck. The gesture supposedly aroused his secretaries, too.

"Sam . . . I can't get any more involved," she whispered unevenly, avoiding his attempt at play.

Taking his time, Sam rose to stand near her. He cupped her chin and looked deeply into her teary, witching eyes. Loving her and meaning every word, he said, "I learned a long time ago that nothing is impossible. Between us, we'll work out the problems. Just don't close any doors, okay?"

With that, Sam kissed her with all the sweetness he felt. Despite Baghdad rubbing against their legs and purring, despite Nikki and Billy cheering in the background, Dallas's lips clung and brushed and warmed his. When her hands slid to his waist and rested there, Sam thought distantly that it was enough for now.

By the middle of February, he noted that the candy maker's bill did not show returned candy credits. He also noticed a new, but definite roundness to Dallas's streamlined body. Sam added the two facts together: Dallas was under definite stress despite the successful job-sharing program. "She'd better be nervous. I play to win," Sam muttered, slamming into his punching bag viciously. "All's fair," he grunted.

Working together every day on designing the child-care center, Sam sensed her studying him. Though she managed to avoid his issue of dating, she seemed to enjoy having him in her home—and knowing his limitations just now, Sam let her. Dallas covered her soft, wounded heart with business trimmings, keeping him on his toes. She let him hold her hand, and to Sam, the gesture signified a beginning.

After the father-daughter Sunbird box lunch, Nikki's glowing report drew Dallas's slow, contemplative stare to Sam. The look held and warmed and promised as she said quietly, "Thank you, Sam."

"Thank you," he returned softly, meaning it.

"Why?" she asked in an uneven whisper as he took her hand.

Lifting it to kiss her chocolate-scented fingers, Sam said simply, "For changing my life. For warming me and caring."

"Oh, Sam," she whispered, looking up into his eyes.

Later, Sam turned her tone over in slow replay. She sounded helpless, vulnerable and too uncertain.

Dallas was as afraid of a relationship as he was.

He wanted her petting him, damn it! He wanted to take care of her even if she didn't want him around. "I want to move back in, is what I want to do," Sam muttered, slamming the bag one last time. "Hell, they adopted me didn't they? I'm not going to turn in my adoption papers without a fight. If Dallas thinks she can put me out in the cold, she's wrong."

The first of March blew gently into Seattle, at odds with the steamy, unvented feeling that Dallas carried within her. Sam knew how to cause stress. He was too sweet, too patient, too adorable, too...everything, including warm and sexy and funny. He gave everyone the impression that though he admired her business skills, he definitely thought of Dallas as his lady.

A man of Sam's size and importance wasn't easily swept aside.

She didn't have the heart to separate him from her cabbage-rose couch, Billy's trucks and Nikki's glowing adoration. Sam really seemed to need her and her family.

"Oh, of course, he knows all that and is using every ounce of it," Dallas snapped, standing up from her office desk. "He knows perfectly well how charming he can be, when to use his dimples and his boxes of candy."

She thought of how Sam had looked into her eyes, claiming her hand and placing it on his chest before she could recover from his sexy stun stare. "Every trick, no matter how low," she muttered, remembering how she'd found her fingers rummaging through the hair on his chest.

She wanted him desperately. He was nothing like T.J.—he was just Sam. Yet somehow, Dallas couldn't let him sweep her off her feet.

This time...this man deserved every bit of thought put into a relationship he obviously wanted.

Tossing the empty candy wrappers into the trash can, Dallas firmly placed the lid on the box of chocolates. She touched the huge elegant red bow, recognizing the blatant symbol of war.

Dallas replaced her pumps with running shoes. She clicked on the electric treadmill she'd had installed in her office. Eight pounds of nervous chocolate binges had lodged on her bust and hips since she'd met Sam. Dallas turned up the pace, walking more quickly. Besides the eight pounds gained she was not sleeping well.

Her mind had wandered in the middle of a class biofeedback experiment, setting up a howl caused by high emotion. Touching base with the questioning expressions of her class, Dallas had found that she had been thinking of Sam's sexy declaration.

Memories of Sam standing in front of the stove, dressed in sweat pants and a stained cotton T-shirt had sent the monitor screaming.

Then there was the hopelessly reverent way he accepted any small thing she'd done for him. Like pasting toilet paper on his untended razor cuts and baking his favorite chocolate cake. Sam never took anything for granted; he took everything personally as if no one had ever cared before.

Thoughts of his kisses started raising unpredictable little constrictions in areas she considered ultrapersonal. "Sexual frustration," she muttered, working harder to drain off her excess energy.

Dallas started thinking about Sam's version of The Three Bears— "And who's been sleeping in my bed?" But lately he'd been tracking her with his smoky eyes, telling her silent stories that caused her to tremble. Of furry navels and gentle, large hands. Of hairy chests and sweet magnolia kisses.

Of lying tangled in the rosebuds sheets while the rain sounded softly against the windowpane. Of pleasure defined by a low, lazy masculine growl.

Dallas wiped the sweat from her forehead and began jogging earnestly. She concentrated on the professional elements of the Brice project.

The job-sharing feature of her plan was a huge success. Though Sam growled about seeing different faces at the same desk every day, he reluctantly admitted liking the cheerful expressions on those faces. Sam did admit when he'd made a mistake—she very much liked that about him.

She planned to add the latchkey program to the child-care center. Sam had suggested the idea, saying he didn't think it was safe for school children to enter empty homes. His latchkey "waiting station" clause also reduced the stress on working parents.

Panting and trying to catch her breath, Dallas shook her head. Sam wanted the plans on his desk in the afternoon to prepare for dinner with the board members and their wives. He wanted her at his side to answer questions wearing "that little basic-black number." "It's good PR to show up at these soirees and push your plans. I want Billy and Nikki to be the first enrolled in the child-care center, Dallas," Sam had stated flatly. "Everyone here knows that I'm...well, attached to them. They'd qualify as my family. I'm not above pulling rank when I have to. Of course, you have the say-so. What do you think?"

She'd thought it was a good idea. Having a creative mind, Sam knew how to balance suggestions with the practical side of his business. Making it clear that he'd accept comments from the staff, Sam was possessive about the program. He did know how to present plans, Dallas admitted. He listened with an intelligent, questioning mind and respected her ideas.

It was the dark side of him that frightened her. *Because she had her own dark side, one she'd never explored until that night.*

Because as gentle as Sam could be, Dallas now feared her own primitive needs when he was near. If he tapped into that fear—Dallas hopped off the treadmill and opened the candy box.

Sucking the bonbon's juice, Dallas thought of the way Sam had been coming to dinner every evening. He often picked up the children, got groceries and had supper waiting on the table when she arrived late at night—and he swept aside her protests with a shrug, "Need to pay you back for the loan." Sam could well afford to pay her back; he was using the tiny loan as an excuse to infiltrate her home and to use her father's power tools. Sam had squashed Beau's interest and she'd never gotten that comparative kiss.

In fact, the last kiss she remembered was Sam's. The memory of it kept her awake at nights, caused her to sink into sweet, sensual dreams and wake up hugging her bed pillows tightly. Closing her eyes, Dallas admitted that Sam knew how to create memorable memories. Every time the Deons celebrated that spring was on its way, kissing in the backyard, the front yard and in the car, Dallas's midsection ached.

Sam wasn't staying at the penthouse now, she was certain of it. Sam had installed his toy train in the center of the company conference table, stating that no one used the space anyway. Judging from the evidence—aftershave on his desk and slacks thrown across a conference chair—Sam's new home was his office. The thought made Dallas's guilt barometer rise.

Sam Loring had that underfed-lonesome-stray-battered-alley-tomcat look pasted all over him. He knew its appeal to her. He knew just how to make her feel like renewing his adoption papers.

But there was more at stake. Big red-flagged, dangerous things like love and commitment and sharing her children and grandchildren. Things like letting her tom-toms riot when the children were asleep. Those were all the things she'd dreamed about at twenty-nine; she had no illusions about white knights carrying off ladies in distress. "Am I in distress?" she asked herself, then answered in a reluctant mumble, "Only when I'm near Sam."

Then there was the awful thing. Like failure looming before her. Remembering her last experience with giving a man one hundred percent, Dallas groaned.

That evening at the dinner for the Board members, Sam's tie was crooked and when Dallas instinctively straightened it, his hands wrapped around her wrists. "I like you fussing over me, sweet pea," he whispered in his sexiest Southern drawl. "Someone will think you care."

"I'm not fussing over you. Anyone would have done the same. And why don't you use that voice with anyone else?" she demanded in a hushed whisper.

"'Cause you're special, sweet pea," Sam whispered back, pulling out his devastating dimples. "Adjusting my tie is a gesture of squaring off female territorial rights. Can't you handle being possessive of me?"

"You're not my territory, Sam. But I can handle anything you can dish out," Dallas said between her teeth.

Sam lifted one eyebrow, the one with the rebellious gray hair. "You think you can, huh?" he asked mockingly. "I can be devious and I'm loaded with chocolate-company stocks."

Recognizing the simmering beat of her tom-toms at Sam's wicked look, Dallas looked away. "Scram. Beat it. Shoo."

Sam's large hand swept down her backside, leaving a trail of warm sensitized flesh. "Not this time," he said in his deadly, means-business tone.

Dallas glanced around the dining room to find her mother watching her intently. Sam traced her frown. "Lisa likes me. The kids like me . . . Bertha misses her parking spot. I want to move back in. I've passed all the hard housebreaking stages now. It would be a perfect chance for you to show me that you can handle anything I can dish out," he said, repeating her words. "I dare you."

"Sam . . ." she warned as his hand fitted neatly into her waist to draw her snugly against him. Aligned with a lean body she wanted to hold, Dallas could feel her temperature rise. Beneath her palm, Sam's heart pounded heavily. "Stop. People are watching."

"Marry me," he said quietly, his gray eyes serious behind his glasses. "Take me away from all this stress. I dare you."

"I tried that, thank you." Dallas forced herself to swallow, moistening a suddenly dry throat.

"Big deal," he said flatly as though sweeping away a bird dropping. "So did I."

"See? We don't even know each other. I don't know anything about why your marriage failed—"

"Is it really important? But I do know a little about T.J. McCall. Enough to know that I'm not paying for another man's idiotic problems."

Sam looked down at her, the angles of his face sharpening with anger. "Lady, I'm not putting up with flack. We worked out the details of my stay at your house, didn't we? We've been working on details of this and that for four months. The bottom line is that we're a good team. And there's more to it than that."

"I'm not going to discuss this here—"

"Then you'd better agree to discuss it in private."

No matter how much she cared for Sam, she wasn't going to let him run her life nor make unreasonable demands. "I don't like ultimatums. Or you'll do what?"

"Or I'll go down on one knee and announce my feelings before this whole dull, boring bunch of desk warmers. Since meeting you, I've become loveable, you know. They wouldn't like you very much if you turned me down. You could make a bad impression that would affect your Brice program. Are you willing to discuss the matter later or not?"

"This sounds like blackmail." Dallas's hands curled into fists.

"Okay, so when I want something, I'm not always nice. I'm tired of waiting for you to give me a fair break." With that last statement fresh on his lips, Sam drew Dallas into his arms. He bent her backward, leaning over her in a Valentino-sheik pose and kissed her.

Underlying the sweetness, his kiss tasted slightly like savage hunger, and Dallas began to answer in kind. His teeth nibbled her bottom lip gently. Though his hands remained quite properly on her waist and shoulders, Dallas had the feeling that they were undressing her and seeking her previously sensitized areas. The heat between them caused her to part her lips, and immediately staking claim, Sam's tongue invaded her mouth.

Locking her arms around him, Dallas sank into Sam's offer. The tender play deepened, and she wondered distantly how anything could improve so much every time he kissed her.

When Dallas was allowed to straighten, she looked into Sam's warm, smoky eyes behind his steamy glasses. She wondered absently what they had been discussing. She stared at Sam's slightly swollen lips helplessly, wanting more—

Lisa wrapped her arm around Dallas's shoulders. "My, my. I think he's got it."

"Got what?" Dallas asked absently, still staring into Sam's flickering, promising gaze behind the steamy lenses.

Lisa laughed low and hugged her daughter. "Whatever it is that puts stars in your eyes. You'd better watch out. Our Sam has his sights set on you. He's not the kind to let you mold on the shelf. I knew this would happen the minute I saw him," she crowed softly before moving toward the buffet table and Edward Swearingen.

Beside Dallas, Sam gave one small sniff. He looked down at her with his untended-battered-and-lonely tomcat look. "Sorry. Guess I'm coming down with a cold. Maybe a virus."

Dallas knew she was falling for the look. The fear from her scarred past rose up instantly and instinctively. Before her, the future loomed like an uncharted abyss. While she knew Sam wasn't her past, the thought that he could be her future badly frightened her. "Take two aspirins, drink juice and go to bed," she said over her shoulder as she quickly walked toward a covey of board members.

"I've got a virus—you," Sam stated clearly behind her. "And I'm needing an immunization shot. Which you should feel obliged to give," he added as he wrapped his arm around her shoulder to forcibly steer her to a forest of potted palms.

"Sam," she protested weakly, bound by his smoky eyes and silent promises.

"Shh, sweet pea. I want you so much." Holding her immobile in the dark secrecy of the shadows, Sam nuzzled her nose with his. When his large, warm hand sought just the right spot low on her spine, Dallas gasped. The wonderful heat she badly wanted to ignore raced through her. While she was fighting her body's unsubtle inclinations to repeat the behind-the-desk scene with a grand finale, Sam nibbled gently on her earlobe. In that lovely, low warm sensual drawl, he whispered, "I love you, sweet pea...I respect you for what you are—who you are—and I think of you as my best friend. I know that if I'm hurting, you'll be there, and I promise to do the same for the rest of my life.... I've never said that to another woman.... Think about it."

Eleven

Easter morning arrived sunlit and spring fresh; Sam arrived on Dallas's front steps ready for church, egg hunting and a family dinner. In his hand was a huge bouquet of daisies and sweet peas; in his eyes was a question Dallas wanted to answer privately.

Sam clearly intended to warm himself in each minute of the day. With evident pride and reverence, he'd walked up the church steps. Later in a quiet moment at the dinner table, he looked across the sweet-pea bouquet to meet her gaze. "Thank you," he murmured quietly, holding Nikki's hand.

Dallas forced herself to look away from him, fearful that she'd throw herself straight into his arms.

Lisa nudged Edward and whispered, "I'll bet dinner that she doesn't make June."

"You're on," he whispered back.

"What's on?" Nikki asked in childishly clear tones.

"You're losing, sweet pea," Sam said quietly, forcing Dallas to look at him when he took her hand.

"Losing what?" Billy asked, carefully isolating his carrots and peas from his "good" food.

The next Thursday night, Lisa called just as Dallas wiped away a tear creeping down her cheek. "You're drowning in those chocolates, Dallas dear," Lisa noted. "Why not just admit that Sam is just perfect for you?"

"Mother—"

"I've never thought of you as a cruel person, Dallas. But Sam is someone very special who obviously adores the children and you. Your father was the love of my heart, dear, and you really mustn't waste any time away from Sam. Every moment is just too precious. Now I've rented you a weekend cottage on Dabob Bay, and I want you to take Sam down there and sort it all out. Work something out before—"

"I do love Sam, Mother," Dallas said quietly, testing the words on her lips. "It's just that I have to find my own way of telling him."

She could almost see her mother's pleased smirk. "You're not stepping through a field of landmines.... See that you do tell him, Dallas dear. Before June, if you could manage it. I like Sam. He's what I call a real man, one you can love with nothing held back. Know what I mean?"

After replacing the receiver, Dallas closed her eyes, forced herself to breathe quietly and wondered just how hard she could love Sam without frightening him. Then, with a feeling of parachuting into the unknown, she picked up the telephone to dial his office.

Sam answered in grizzly-bear tones. "Loring."

After a deep breath, Dallas said "Hello."

"What's wrong, Dallas?" Sam asked, his deep tone anxious. "Do you need me? I knew the kids were eating too much candy.... I'm coming over right away—"

"Sam?"

"What?"

"I want kisses at midnight, warm hands to hold when I'm lonely, pleased-grizzly-bear growls after lovemaking, hot-buttered bagels in the morning, someone sweet and tender holding me while the rain runs down the windowpanes, someone to take care of when he's cold and lonely, someone to take care of me when I'm down, someone to run power tools at midnight and touch me like I'm the only woman he's ever loved. I'm talking about a sweet-talking man with a Southern drawl and dimples who makes me want to never let him go. About being together in the good times and the bad. About our family going to church and Easter dinners, laundry on Saturday nights, and baking chocolate cakes for a man who really appreciates them. About fighting and making up, and trusting and sharing, and loving for years to come. I'm talking about putting a baby in a hand-crafted cradle and watching the children grow up together.... How am I doing, Sam?" she asked breathlessly.

After a long pause that caused Dallas's fingers to grip the phone too tightly, Sam said quietly, "You'd better know what you're talking about, lady."

"Meet me tomorrow night at the bay, Sam. I'll send you the directions. And we'll negotiate clauses."

"Pretty damned hard to negotiate with a virus," Sam stated roughly. "They get you every time."

Dallas quietly replaced the telephone with the definite feeling that Sam was ready to tear down doors to get to the one woman he wanted. And she was the only woman he wanted. She allowed herself a delicate, pleased smirk—to be Sam's woman was quite a feeling—his mate when all the negotiations were completed.

Bertha was already parked at the cabin when Dallas arrived. The low, gray clouds swept over the rough waters of the bay; the fine mist curled about her as she walked up the path to the cabin. She smiled softly, thinking that the weathered cabin with smoke rising from the chimney reminded her of Sam. While it appeared seasoned and cold, the cabin withstood the fierce elements, and comfort and warmth waited for her inside...just like Sam.

He opened the door, the lantern light behind him outlining his body. With the wind riffling his hair and dressed in a cream knit sweater and jeans, Sam watched her intently. He took her case and slowly placed it on the floor, still looking at her. Straightening to his full height, he said tightly, "Tell me you love me."

When she took off her jacket, nervously running her hands down her sweater and jeans, Sam demanded stiffly, "Okay. Then tell me you want me."

Dallas lifted an eyebrow at him, teasingly. "Could we go at this in stages?" she asked, knowing that Sam had his own ideas about the proper stages of negotiating a lifelong contract.

"Nope," he stated flatly, then scooped her up in his arms and carried her to the bed. "I want it all now. And later. And then more. In between, we'll sort out the clauses."

When he placed her gently on the bed, Dallas traced the fierce line between his eyebrows. "I do love you, Sam."

He sat beside her slowly, brushing her hair away from her cheek, his hands trembling. "You took your sweet time."

Carefully placing his large hands along her cheeks, Sam kissed her tenderly, making promises that would last forever. "Don't get any ideas that you can cancel this contract," he murmured unevenly against her cheek as he eased down on the bed beside her.

With trembling hands, they slowly undressed each other, making promises with caresses and gentle kisses and lingering gazes. Folding her carefully against him, Sam smoothed the line of her back gently. Dallas moved closer, raising her arms to hold him tightly, fitting herself against the man who would last through the hard times. Against his ear, she whispered a warning, "Hold on, Sam."

He chuckled warmly, knowingly. "So that's how it's going to be?"

"Yes," she managed as they became one, bound by love and the future waiting for them.

Sam moved against her hungrily, searching for her mouth and claiming it. Without fear, she gave him what he sought.

He tasted of the hunger driving her; his heart pounded beneath her hand, her own special tom-toms begging her to incite a riot.

Diving into what he offered, what he would take and give back with the honesty she demanded, Dallas drew him into the magic of a hot, Southern, sweet-pea-scented-Appalachia-air magnolia night.

Trailing kisses across her damp cheeks, Sam nibbled at her lips. She traced his mouth with hers, blending the intimacy with a rough hunger that caused Sam to growl low in his throat.

The sound quickened Dallas's internal tom-tom beat and her hands slid down his back. Drawing Sam deeper, Dallas showed him all the heat within her, all the love just for him.

He accepted her gift, lifting her higher, and while Dallas fought the need to cry out, Sam gently bit her earlobe and whispered roughly, "I'm here. I'll always be here—I love you, Dallas."

No longer fighting, Dallas stepped out onto her private ledge and went free-falling into Sam's love.

Later, he held her, bringing her back to earth and the cabin with sweet Southern drawls and quieting hands. "Help," he teased, running a large, open hand down his newly claimed territory. "Tell me you love me again."

Knowing that Sam really worked to get his way when denied, Dallas grinned up at him, smiled widely, and said, "Nope."

"You're tough, Pendragon. But I"m determined," he returned with a matching, teasing grin. "You'll tell me—"

"No way," she murmured before his lips sealed hers in a sweet, devastating sexy kiss. "Well, maybe—" she added as he drew her over him.

Epilogue

"The kid is a demanding tyrant," Sam said in a pleased daddy tone, placing his son in his cradle after a midnight feeding.

"He'll start sleeping better once you stop showing him off," Dallas teased as Sam bent to kiss her. During the seven weeks since baby's birth, Sam had definitely leashed his kissing powers. Dallas, after shedding her candy and "new-mother" pounds, didn't want any sensual stress to cause a repeat of her chocolate-covered-cherry's eating binge. With quiet determination, she had baked Sam's favorite chocolate cake and asked her mother to take Billy and Nikki for a weekend in the mountains.

While Sam turned off the lights in their new home, Dallas plotted to seduce him. She lit candles in their bedroom, the hardwood floor catching the glow that washed over their king-size four-poster bed. Dallas watched her husband stroll back to bed with the air of Baghdad's male this-is-my-kingdom confidence.

In the year and a half since their wedding ceremony, Sam had never complained about family life. She loved him deeply and was confident in his love. Sam really listened to her, often giving her ideas for improving her business and ideas—except for the Whammy. The really nice thing about Sam was that he did wonderful, personal things for her ego. And he demonstrated his love in any way he could.

But Sam had a tendency to be a little too careful. Especially when she'd been pregnant and he'd looked at her with such love and concern that she'd ached for him. He'd been there during Brent's delivery, then had quietly seemed to go limp and helpless after the birth.

She smiled as the candlelight softened the desire in his expression. Sam had built the new house as a gift of love, yet never was too busy for the children, who adored him. The toy train and "guy stuff" occupied a place of honor in the family room, and Sam had whittled a tiny female engineer just for Nikki.

Pausing beside the bed, Sam looked down at Dallas tenderly. "What's the candlelight occasion?"

Taking his hand and lacing her fingers with his, Dallas savored a game that she knew they would play forever. "You're going to tell me you love me tonight."

Sam frowned, a tense muscle moving in his cheek. "I must tell you that at least twice a day. I even call you at your offices—" Then his frown deepened, shielding what Dallas thought to be high hope. "Did the doctor say it was okay to...?"

She smiled wickedly, tugging lightly on his hand to urge him into the rosebud sheets and her waiting tom-tom beats.

When Sam slid into the rosebuds, she fitted her naked body to his, wrapped her arms around him and nibbled at his ear. She'd found that Sam's earlobes were definitely susceptible to nibbling. "Tell me you love me," she urged, allowing her hands to caress Sam's powerful, hair-flecked anatomy.

"Make me," he challenged, laughing up at her. "Be gentle," he whispered a moment later.

Even later, he managed to say "Okay. I love you."

*   *   *   *   *

Take 4 bestselling love stories FREE

Plus get a FREE surprise gift!

Silhouette Special Edition

proudly presents
the long-awaited "prequel" volume of

★ **LOVE AND GLORY** ★

by
LINDSAY McKENNA

Dawn of Valor

In the summer of '89, Silhouette Special Edition premiered three
novels celebrating America's men and women in uniform: LOVE
AND GLORY, by bestselling author Lindsay McKenna. Featured
were the proud Trayherns, a military family as bold and patriotic
as the American flag—three siblings valiantly battling the threat
of dishonor, determined to triumph . . . in love and glory.

Now, discover the roots of the Trayhern brand of courage, as
parents Chase and Rachel relive their earliest heartstopping
experiences of survival and indomitable love, in

Dawn of Valor, Silhouette Special Edition #649.

This February, experience the thrill of LOVE AND GLORY—from
the very beginning!

DV-1

Silhouette Books